I0722746

for Virginia and Anastasia

STRAYS LIKE US

a short story collection by Garrett Francis

ABOUT THIS BOOK

Strays Like Us **is a collection of ten standalone stories exploring what it means to grow up in America.**

"A significant talent, fearless, natural, and hard to classify."
  -David Ebershoff, author of *The Danish Girl*

"A power house of a fiction writer. Poetic and raw, imaginative and real, Garrett is blessed with a literary talent that many can only dream of."
  -Claudia Befu-Ibarra, author of *Story Voyager*

"Garrett Francis' fiction isn't only immersive, but is also tremendously cinematic. You literally feel yourself in a spectacular movie."
  -Nadia Gerassimenko, author of *when hope writes*

"One of the author's greatest strengths is in writing characters that are truly complex. He never does exactly what you'd expect, and for me, that's what makes them so human and Francis so good at what he does."
  -Amazon Reader

Copyright © Garrett Francis, 2025.

All rights reserved. No parts of this book may be copied, distributed, or published in any form without permission from the publisher. For permissions contact: authorgarrettfrancis@gmail.com

This is a work of fiction in which all events and characters in this book are completely imaginary. Any resemblance to actual people is entirely coincidental.

ISBN: 978-1-7338171-4-1

Published by 5626 Press

TABLE OF CONTENTS

TRISOMY

AFTER MONTHS ON the tracks together, Derrick waved at me for the first time tonight. He'd been jogging and jogging, not a care in the world, but then had just stopped cold ten feet away and thrust his arm into the sky. He waved his hand back and forth slow, real slow, as if he'd been talking himself through each step but then hit this one and found that he liked it. The feeling, the motion. He's been on my heels ever since, smiling, staring, hopping over tracks, smiling, staring. God, that kid can stare.

"Quit bothering Gary!" Jack shouts to Derrick. He yells as if he'd convinced himself a while ago that inside voices don't work with his son, mostly with authority but also with traces of venom.

Derrick stands still. He looks at Jack, opens his mouth, tucks his tongue behind his lower lip. Looks like a tiny pink ball he isn't sure how to bounce yet. I expect him to say something. Because I've heard him talk. He talks just fine. But he stands there, much closer to scared than he is to angry.

"You're not bothering me, Derrick," I say. I want it to be consoling. Have no idea if I'm doing it right, if there is a right way. I wave at Jack. "No bother at all," I yell.

Jack starts walking towards the front of the train. "We have to get moving," he says.

Derrick tightens the stocking cap over his ears, then takes a few cautious steps toward me. Then a few the other way, unsure of where he's supposed to go. I point at the back of the train and tell him that's where I'll be.

"You should probably go with your dad," I say.

Derrick doesn't think twice. Sprints to catch Jack but falls down. Rolls this way and that before pushing himself to his feet and dusting the snow from his jacket. I assume it happens often, the falling. He's come here with scabs on his chin and palms. Bouts with gravel, with asphalt, with sticks and brush. No way Jack does that to him. He gets pissed, sure, and he might shout, but never would he hurt his son, not like that. If there is one thing I'm certain of, it's that.

Tonight is the usual, from Grand Rapids to Detroit and back. We'll drop off or pick up freight—top of the line scrap and chemicals whose value keeps plummeting—at stations between. It once was a four or five man job in lake effect conditions like this, before GLX cut all routes to two. Before Tim and Joaquin started playing grab-ass with uppers and McGillcuddy's. Before the two of them derailed. Before they booted me to the back of the train. Before picket signs were aimed at my chest. Before GLX started listening to the green talk, before the protestors, before the activists, before the seas of button-ups and slacks.

They got their way. The transition to everything electric has been inching along for over a year now. Neither Jack or I know what will become of us when the conversion is through. No idea if the union will find us worth fighting for, two single men with pensions, with years of knowledge rocketing toward being obsolete, with experience that would require retooling. Or if there will be a union at all. I know Jack has been looking for other jobs. I have too. Mechanic, plumber, maintenance man, none that whet the appetite. But, instead of churning ourselves into the deep, Jack and I have been trying to make the run as enjoyable as we can. A last hurrah, if that's what it comes down to.

We've even started to bring our own walkie talkies on board. Jack just showed up with them one day, batteries and all. A no-no, from GLX's viewpoint. All communication onboard is supposed to take place through their radio system. For safety reasons, reps have touted before, without defining whom they're keeping safe by doing so. The answer is GLX, of course. Dialogue through their system means eavesdropping. It means analysis. It means evidence.

The first few times we used the walkie talkies, Jack would talk mostly about Derrick. He'd tiptoe his mind toward Wanda. But that changed. Started talking sports, and fishing, and cars we can't afford, things he and I talk about to this day. Two things have deterred us from that pattern: Molly, the night dispatcher, who Jack likes to pick on over the train's radio, and truckers. For a spell, we'd highjack their frequencies. Eavesdrop. Harass them a bit, offer some spice to the night. A conversation we picked up last week was with a female driver who felt she'd been dealt a bad hand.

"Jerry left this morning." She sighed. "Again. Just took the TV, his antlers, his shirts, and that was it. Out the fuckin' door." She sniffled and I'd bet a hefty amount she intended for the other driver to hear it.

I was content just listening. She did have a story. And she did have a voice, just like Molly's: soothing, even in tragedy. One that belongs in a choir.

But Jack hopped on. "You think you got it rough?" he said. There was a pause afterward that made me keep picturing that question finding its way through his teeth. Then Jack gave her an earful.

I don't think the woman listened long before switching channels. But Jack just kept going. He vented. And I was glad he did. Something about life and death, love and loss, needs and wants, all blurred together. It made me think of the things we bottle up, the pressure it causes, the weight we teach ourselves to manage through routine. Made me question my own life for a bit, the gates I tend to keep shut.

There's a knock at the door. I look out the window and see Derrick. Spit hangs from his lower lip. The cold has painted his cheeks scarlet. I open the door and he says something I register as, "I asked Dad if I could ride with you and he said I could so I came back here."

"Come on in," I say, not out of pity, or some sense of obligation. I like Derrick. Watching him decipher his surroundings is like nothing else I've experienced. More than a candy shop. More than an amusement park. Absolute wonder. "Tight quarters back here but we'll manage."

My walkie talkie chirps.

"Gary," Jack says. After I acknowledge, he says, "Derrick said he wanted to ride with you for a change. That okay?"

I watch Derrick find the lever for the horn. He wiggles it a bit. The horn goes off. Derrick didn't expect the sound. He covers his ears.

I bring the lever back. "We'll have some fun back here."

"Please don't let him do that," Jack says.

We start moving. Derrick jolts toward the door, his train legs much weaker than mine. I'm hesitant to touch him, though. "Take a seat," I say, and point to the chair near the control panel. Which he sits in soon enough, hands searching for something to hold.

Jack told me once how bad Derrick's temper tantrums can be, told me there doesn't even need to be a traceable cause to them. They just happen. Said they got worse when he turned four, the first time he tried to run away. Said the sounds Derrick made that day reminded him of a piglet being carried by its back legs. Those sounds can shake a man. A week or so afterward, Jack drew up miniature stop signs for each door in their house as a visual cue to Derrick that he couldn't leave.

I've never drawn a thing in my life, let alone keep it somewhere back here. He doesn't seem too interested in running away at the moment, though. Now that we're zipping along, he isn't interested in me. Or the controls. He stays seated, looks out the window, studies the blur we leave behind.

###

Jack and Wanda had no idea Derrick was going to be born with Down syndrome. I guess doctors could've caught it beforehand, in the ultrasound, or in some blood test, or whatever. Could've placed in Jack's hands the study material he would days after Derrick was born tape on the wall of the engine we share. The one that says, "Nondisjunction results in an embryo with three copies of chromosome twenty-one instead of the usual two. The extra chromosome is replicated in every cell of the body, which is called Trisomy twenty-one."

But they didn't catch it. According to Jack, the doctor told them after he'd inspected Derrick, pushed his eyelids up, opened his palms. According to Jack, he and Wanda had sat there quietly, but only for a few seconds before kissing

Derrick and hugging one another. According to Jack, no kind of syndrome was going to get in the way of love.

Jack does have it rough as a single father though. Being an engineer doesn't mix well. Neither do the nightshifts. But he's tried to make it work. Takes Derrick to movies on his days off, sometimes to church. Tried putting him in school once, I guess. As it was told, there was some scuffle over a game of checkers that resulted in Derrick shrieking like a banshee. Didn't hit the other kid, didn't throw the checkerboard. Just shrieked something fierce. So the teachers, either not wanting to take care of it, or just not knowing how, called Jack to pick him up.

"They have special classes for kids like him," Jack told me months back, after a run. He was too exhausted to huff and puff, to show any kind of frustration. "But I don't want that." What followed wasn't what I'd call an explanation. To be honest, I don't know what I'd call it. Jack just argued with himself aloud. Pros and cons, slanting the weight of things until any sort of solution was so far buried that he'd forgotten entirely what the argument was about.

"He's been on my goddamn sleep schedule since then. Did I tell you that?" He even forced a chuckle. "I didn't, did I? My mom feeds him, reads to him, tucks him in when she sees his eyes shut. But he isn't asleep. No, no way, not for a second. All night he waits for me to come home and it's only when I'm there that he curls up on the couch and passes out." Jack sighed. "Gets up before I do too."

I can't remember if I responded or not. I don't think so. Probably just stood there with the same feelings I still have, stuck on that image of Derrick at school, wishing Wanda was still around to have a say, knowing that there is a whole lot of love in wanting to protect your child. A whole lot of love in not wanting him to come home crying every day, or needing to be picked up, singled out. But, goddamn, does it squash a lot of opportunities for the kid.

That's when I proposed Jack bring Derrick with us on the route. My reasoning wasn't strong. Just pity I mistook for empathy, for Jack, for Derrick, imagining the poor kid awake in bed, twirling his thumbs, eager to greet his dad at the door. Detained by those stop signs.

At least get him out of the house, I thought, as he and I waited for Jack to come around with school. Let him see a sliver of the world.

Took some convincing on my end, considering that it's illegal for us to have him on board. Derrick would be unwanted freight for a transitioning company. Derrick would be a liability that is not to be seen or heard.

But he's been with us every shift in the seven weeks since.

###

Derrick looks through the window. At what, I'm not sure, and I don't think it matters. I'm just surprised at how quiet he has been. I know he sometimes rides the entire route in tears. Says the light up front makes him sad. Even after Jack turns it off, he cries. Because Derrick hasn't told us why that is just yet, we chalk it up to the fact that not every moment is happy for him. Because it's the truth. Another truth: not every moment is happy for anyone. Derrick has just been given the gift of having fewer ways to filter his emotions. If he's happy, he'll giggle. If he's confused, his face will coil like wire until it becomes a question mark. If he's angry, he'll shriek. He doesn't suppress. He doesn't hide.

Makes me wonder what I'd be like if I couldn't conceal my feelings, if I'd have a wife and kids with a house in the suburbs instead of a lonely one bedroom kitty corner to that Mexican market on Leonard. Maybe I'd have a son that Derrick could play with. We could take them to Garfield

Park and they could swing on the swingset, or struggle with monkeybars, or just run together for hours.

"How's everything back there?" Jack says to me over the walkie talkie.

Derrick turns to me as he hears Jack's voice. He smiles.

"Everything's good," I say.

Derrick reaches for the walkie talkie.

"I think someone wants to talk to you," I say, then hand the walkie talkie to Derrick.

He just looks at it, brings the speaker to his ear like it's a phone.

"No, no, no," I say. I tell him to bring the device to his mouth. "Then you push this button down. After you hear the beep, you start talking, but you gotta keep that button held down."

Derrick nods and presses the button, then talks. "Hi Dad!" Derrick says. He keeps the button held.

"Now let go," I say.

He nods and lets go of the button, grinning as if to say, "I should have known that."

"Are you being a good boy back there?" Jack asks.

Derrick hits the button once but lets go too soon and says, "I'm being really good, Dad," before I remind him he has to hold it down. He repeats himself.

"Well, you just keep being a good boy, okay?"

"I will, Dad," he says, like any kid would say it. He has the process down now.

"Okay, now give the walkie talkie back to Gary."

Derrick nods again, then hands the walkie talkie to me.

"Smart little guy, Jack," I tell him. I want it to be a hint that maybe Derrick can handle more, that maybe it'd be best to try school one more time, that he'd quickly learn how to be around other children. But I'm no expert. Maybe being able to work a walkie talkie proves nothing.

"I'll see you soon." It's all he says.

A former coworker of ours once called Derrick a murderer while on lunch. I'd only known Jack for a couple months at the time so I didn't take much offense. Because it wasn't entirely untrue. Wanda died three days after Derrick was born because of what Jack called amniotic fluid embolism. Sometimes I wonder if Jack finds comfort in big words like that, if the way they roll off his tongue calms him. I wonder because, in the years I've known him, he has gone on with the story, bit by bit. Said her uterus had torn during labor. Said amniotic fluid had seeped back into her bloodstream. Said that it isn't good. Hard to detect. Hard to fix.

It wasn't until three years or so after Wanda died that Jack and I grew closer, our conversations evolving from GLX talk to talk about life, our upbringings, our teams. He started inviting me to his house. Not often, maybe once a month to drink a beer and watch whatever sport was in season. He still hadn't come out of it yet. The house was messy. Dishes heaped in the sink, on the counter, clothes trailing down the hallway and into Jack's bedroom. He kept a box of diapers on the coffee table, beside medical magazines and children's books. None of it distracted me as much as the entertainment center though.

It was almost a shrine to Wanda. A doily with her name sewn in turquoise. Dangling jewelry. A photo here, a photo there. One of her in a bikini and big sunglasses, all tanned up. Another where she was pregnant, a Woodland Mall Santa Claus crouched and whispering to her belly. Just photo after photo. Different dresses, different earrings, always something different. There was one I especially liked, a grainy one. Could've been before a high school dance. Jack had shaggy hair then, just stood toward the back of some dark dining room. And there was Wanda, hands on her hips, head tilted in confusion, amusement, something about Jack worth smiling at. Her dress wasn't anything special, wasn't too revealing, cut below the neck and showing her collarbone. But that smile. Those teeth. That olive oil skin framed by the crimson on her thin lips. Reminded me of someone I thought I loved once. Until I met Derrick, that's where my eyes would go, that picture.

We pull into the Lansing yard. Weather's worse here. Can't see the stars, can't see the treetops. Even the lampposts are wrapped in gray, yellow bulbs blotted orange by the wind's attempts to swirl snow into wool. On the ground, grimacing men walk along each side of the cars, bodies angled, a series of parka hoods spearing the wind. They take our car off first to allow for presorting, so the connector from Detroit to Cleveland won't have to have all its freight taken off and arranged again. Derrick doesn't know what to make of being uncoupled. He has never been this close to these men. Maybe he's sniped glances at them before but I doubt it. Jack probably maneuvers with one hand while keeping Derrick low with the other, crouched as if he were at war and taking cover behind a mound of sod.

If the men outside were to see him, I don't know what would happen. They could keep it between us, ask about him over the radio instead of reporting it directly to their superior, having someone punished. Or, they could go gung-ho. Jolt the message up the chain. Rat. I don't need to ask Jack over the walkie talkie to know that neither of us want to find out which route they'd choose. So I position myself as a shield of Derrick and move as the men do, from the east window to the west.

"You're all right, Derrick," I say.

I want to put my hand on his shoulder to calm him down but I know I shouldn't turn around, shouldn't expose our liability. And, again, I don't know if touching him is the right thing to do in this moment. Maybe Derrick would panic, dig his half-bitten fingernails into my hands and wrists, figure out the door and fly like a hawk into the night. We stay like this. For a while we do, quiet and shuffling.

When the added freight is ready, Jack backs up into our car until it latches. This time is no different than others: the noise is short-lived, but sharp, deafening. Our car glides back a ways. But once the train's groaning fades, I hear Derrick crying behind me. Low, controlled sobs. I turn around and crouch, tell Derrick to do the same. He squints his eyes and opens his mouth wide. No sound comes out.

We're yanked forward. Derrick's back slings against the door. And he shouts. The shout soon becomes a moan. Something deeper, something from his gut, until his throat clutches it, until the moan becomes a shriek.

"Shh, shh, shhhh," I say with my finger to my mouth. My eyes are reeling, from Derrick to the window, from the window to Derrick. Derrick-window-Derrick-window. "It's all right, it's all right." It isn't. We aren't. We are confined. We cannot hear. We can barely see.

I hesitantly cradle his back and guide him to my seat. He's shaking and still crying, but quieter now, moans drowned by the engine. Tears slide to his lips.

"You're a big boy, Derrick. You're doing great. It'll be over soon. It will." I want to wipe the tears for him and apologize, but for what?

The walkie talkie chirps. "Everything okay back there?" Jack asks.

I look at Derrick. He wipes his eyes. He bites his nails. Nerves, that's why they're jagged. "Can I talk to you outside for a minute?"

"Yeah, sure."

I tell Derrick I'll be right back. He tugs at my jacket sleeve as I open the door. I turn around, force a smile. I touch his shoulder, repeat what I just said.

"I promise."

My shadow is lost in the murk of the night. Blown snow clings to my beard, then melts. Most of the grimacing men have made it back to their stations, the scent of the cigarettes I know them to be smoking lost somewhere in the wind. The nearby stretch of highway is empty at this hour. I see Jack up ahead, his faded red jacket first, then his boots, striding unintentionally to the engine's rhythm. He meets me near halfway.

"What's up?" he asks. His hood is up. I can only see his chin and lips. No need to find his eyes. "You leave him alone in there?"

"He's fine, Jack." Far from it. Isn't a matter of whether he should or should not live in isolation, in fear, with apology. He just can't. Those are three piss-poor options.

Jack takes his hood off. His eyes are narrow, his cheeks smudged pink. "What's up then?"

"I want to know what you're going to do with him."

"What do you mean?"

"I mean that he doesn't belong here, Jack." I try real hard to maintain eye contact but lose the battle and let them wander to a lone semi merging onto the highway. "He's just a kid. He needs to be around other kids." I want to tell him how Derrick reacted to these men. I want to tell him about the nerves, the fingernails, things he already knows but continues to ignore.

Jack starts walking to the front of the train. His voice becomes distant. "You know, I should've known this would happen." He turns around, points at me. "What, an hour or two with him alone and you think you can criticize my parenting? Him being here was your idea in the first place." Jack spits on the ground. "Fuck you, Gary."

It isn't the first time someone has said that to me. It is the first time Jack has, though, and it hurts. A snakebite, twisting its way beneath my skin. But this is bigger than me and him. Bigger than his words. I follow him for ten feet or so.

"Let's talk about it at breakfast, in front of him," I yell. "Ask him what he wants to do."

But Jack ignores me. Walks off, hood up, back into what he has made bleak.

The day I did meet Derrick, he was crying a couple rooms over while Jack and I watched a Tigers game. I'd never been around a kid with Down syndrome before. Didn't know how to respond when Jack brought him out to the living room. Didn't know how to stare back. It isn't just Derrick though, it isn't just Down syndrome; I've never known how to act with children, not even my nieces and nephews. What to say, how to play with them. I want to interact. I do. But I just feel like I'd hurt them somehow. That I'd disappoint. Too tall, too boring, too damaged. Check, check and check.

Jack didn't tell Derrick to be quiet or anything. Cradled him, shushed him, waited for the episode to pass. He didn't drink anymore that day, not even a sip, just let his beer can sweat dark rings into the end table. After what he'd been through I was surprised, and impressed, that Jack hadn't turned to alcohol. I was proud of him. The place was dirty, sure, but empty bottles of vodka weren't strewn about, no whiskey, not even wine. Turning to such a vice, to such relief, would've been easy. But he hadn't turned to anything. Maybe those big words, that stack of knowledge, but that was all. Heaped the remaining weight on his shoulders, and it showed. He'd become thinner, a little paler than when I'd first met him, edgier than he once was.

I remember the game went to a commercial and Jack looked around the room awkwardly, trying to find conversation in the ceiling. "You hear from Evelyn yet?" he finally asked.

I remember this because he was the first to ask. I remember this because I wasn't ready to talk about her. Just hearing her name made my throat swell. "I haven't," I said. But I had. She'd called me the night before. Talked quietly, like someone else was in the room. Said I'd like Pittsburgh.

"What does she want to do out there again?"

Though I didn't say it, I'd convinced myself then that the obvious answer was men. Lots of men. And bars. And men. Truth was that she'd log fifty-plus hours per week at the only firm that would hire a girl from the mitten, find a banker that would cut that in half, marry him and have three kids. Truth was I'd bought a .357 without knowing what I'd use it for.

"Don't really wanna talk about it, Jack," I said. I was relieved when shortly after the game came back from commercial.

The top of the inning went by in silence, save for the commentator's banter. I'd glance at Derrick as each batter maxed the count and find him staring at me. That kid really can stare. Made me very uncomfortable back then, very nervous, like he was trying to find something in my face. A key, a clue, a weakness, I don't know. Tried to play peek-a-boo with him. Covered my face with my hands, moved them to the side, widened my eyes. He didn't like it one bit. Hid his face in Jack's chest. I apologized.

"No need to apologize," Jack said. "You're figuring one another out is all."

Then Derrick hopped off of Jack's lap and ran into his room. He came back out dragging a plastic train track across the carpet, the train still on it but wavering to beat hell.

Jack sighed. "Not now, Derrick."

Derrick dragged the set over to me, placed it at my feet like a gift. Even tugged at my bootlace. When neither Jack or I got on the floor with him, Derrick guided the train around the circle, not saying a word.

"Derrick, what does the train say?" I asked him. Had thought about it for a while before asking, considered a bunch of other questions and tones before settling on that one. Baby talk, small talk. Dumb things.

But Derrick smiled at me, opened his mouth as wide as he could and let out a long-winded howl that, though it sounded more like some wailing coyote, I took to be the horn of the train.

Jack laughed. The laugh faded into a smile, one I thought should last longer than just that afternoon. Not then, but later, when I hit red light after red light on my drive home, I remember hoping it marked some kind of change. In him, in me, in Derrick. A groove found. A gap bridged. A corner turned. I'm happy I was there for that. I am. I think of that moment often.

###

"You guys are about fifteen minutes out of Detroit, right?" Molly says over the radio, her voice lower than normal. I picture her swiveling in her chair, black hair haloed by the headset, Big Mac wrapper balled on her desk.

"Aww, what's the matter, Molly?" Jack asks. "Boyfriend leave ya?"

Jack talks to her like this sometimes, tries to be playful. He isn't good at it. Sounds forced. But I want to cheer him on with Molly. To say he deserves it may be shallow but I like to think he deserves her, that they could make something work. Maybe not marriage and picket fences, but something.

Molly comes back with her usual vinegar. "I don't have a boyfriend, thank you very much." That voice, even doused in sarcasm, just sings. Hints at youth, says her soul is not yet rusted.

"Yeah, yeah, yeah, we're close," Jack tells her.

The radio is silent for a few seconds, until Molly, her voice low again, asks, "Is someone else on board with you tonight?"

Which rattles me. I look at Derrick, who stares at the door behind me.

"I got a call in from Lansing saying someone saw an additional passenger in the window."

I sigh, then say into my radio, "We do have an additional passenger tonight, Molly. Derrick's on board. Derrick's with us." It's time. And Jack sure as hell wasn't going to.

I turn my radio down so I can't hear either one of them, then grab the walkie talkie. "I'm silenced, Jack." It's the first thing I've said to him since Lansing. But I want to let Jack and Molly talk without Derrick or me listening. I don't care what they talk about. Him, me, them, the consequences, the weather, doesn't matter, as long as they talk. All I want to do is watch the boy.

Because Lake Erie has yet to pull winter's veil over Detroit, Derrick has rediscovered his amazement with this end of the train. He watches the tracks fade behind us,

endless, indistinguishable from the next rung if it weren't for
the side streets, their glow, their bicycle racks and bent signs.
And if I was able to help in this amazement, I'm happy with
that. I'm happy imagining that Jack and Molly are hitting it
off, that they're setting up a date where he opens the door
for her at a fancy restaurant and then takes her for a walk
around the city. They could hold hands, they could hug, they
could move forward from there, see where it takes the three
of them. Because there is room. In all of their lives, there is.

Skyscrapers come into view. The Marriott. Cadillac
Tower tucked somewhere in there. Others I've never known
the names of. The flashing red bulbs of railroad crossing
signs begin to pulse onto the hoods of stopped sedans.

"Go ahead," Jack says over the walkie talkie. And I can
hear it in his voice: he stifled a laugh to say so.

I've been thinking about this for a while. "Come here,"
I say to Derrick.

He's hesitant, but eventually takes the two steps to the
control panel.

"Give me your hand."

When he gives me his hand I can feel that trench on
his palm the doctor felt, the trench Jack said most born with
Down syndrome have. There is no message in this trench,
no sermon. In fact, I don't know how it makes me feel, and I

probably won't for some time. But I am not sorry for him. I am not sad for him. Or angry. Not at all.

I place Derrick's hand on the horn's lever and make sure his fingers wrap all the way around. "Push it forward," I say.

He does. The horn blares. He smiles. I smile. He bounces my hand up and down.

"Get ready," I say. "We'll do it again in just a second."

I tell myself to howl when he does.

DON'T SIT STILL

0 MILES – STERLING HEIGHTS, MICHIGAN

Winona would do this.

266 MILES – GARY, INDIANA

"Coffee?"

I nodded. I watched the waitress pour too much. The cup overflowed. A brown puddle rippled across the saucer beneath.

"East or west?"

"Heading west."

"Alone?" I didn't appreciate the tone she took when asking, some strange blend of surprise and jealousy, that I wasn't settling, that she hadn't done something similar, that my journey, unlike hers, wouldn't start and end in Gary.

"Yeah."

"How old are you?"

"Eighteen."

"Really?"

"Yeah."

"Would've guessed sixteen."

Thanks. Before I could say anything else, she'd hurried to a man seated in one corner of the restaurant, also alone. He wore a pressed blue button-up and a baseball cap as black as his beard. While speaking with me, she'd appeared to have had her youth beaten from her bones like dust from a rug; for this man, though, she was more than capable of sashaying through the restaurant as if she were twenty-five. I watched her giddily take his order and half-pirouette away from his table and back toward me.

"Be with you in a second, hun," she told me as she passed by, on the way to the server station. She even touched my shoulder, like we'd known each other for longer than sixty seconds.

It was comforting, I have to admit.

I took a moment to study the man. He had short legs, stood five-six, maybe five-seven, with a strong neck and triceps that stretched his shirt taut. For a moment, I imagined him setting several records at his small high school, crowdsurfing down a long hallway with one exit, this top dog in assists and touchdowns or pins and pussy. But he had few victories now, if any. There was no winning shot anymore, no skirt to lift up, no panties to nervously pull aside, no bra to unclasp. His sad stare out the front window said so. A life of nostalgia, constant reminders of his peak.

The waitress clicked her pen. "What can I get ya?"

"Two eggs over easy, links, wheat toast. Side of pancakes."

"Big appetite."

I nodded.

The waitress scurried to the man once more and giggled like a cheerleader that had botched the squad's routine with an unsynchronized kick. It made me wonder if she'd always wanted to belong to him, if they'd been classmates, if he'd charmingly cheated off of her C- exams. But, even as he spoke, the man kept looking out the window, as if he were some bird no longer satisfied scouring frosted dirt for worms.

444 MILES – DAVENPORT, IOWA

Winona may have always been a mirage. Glowing in doorways of movie theaters, on the trodden grass of our Dodge Park, Lake Huron's shore, on this motel room's dark blue ceiling. Skin the shade of coconut. Stunning. Radiant.

San Diego now. With Francis.

Francis. Francis. I'd never vomited over a name before. But there she was, ankle deep in the Pacific, skin clear as ever, smooth, sun-bleached hair. Appearing free in uploaded mirages. 129 likes.

Uploads do nothing at all to kill love; eleven months of them can't kill that. Mere scabs picked at. Dead skin balled beneath fingernails.

802 MILES – LINCOLN, NEBRASKA

Mom called today and wanted to have a conversation for once. She asked how I was and I told her fine. She asked how the car was holding up and I said fine.

"Eating enough?"

"I'm fine. Going through a drive-thru (I'll take a number four with Sprite, please)."

"We miss you already, that smile of yours."

That wasn't true. I wouldn't actually be missed for months, not until the holidays, the only time her actions mirror her intent. But I told her I miss them too, even Maggie, our bloodhound, which wasn't true either. I miss you should have more weight, but it doesn't, not from her. From Winona, sure; I miss you would've meant more than something then.

"I heard a squeak—are the breaks okay? I can wire you some money."

"They're fine, Mom. Everything's fine (thanks)."

"You're sure?"

"Yes. I'm going to eat now."

"Ok. Be safe, I love you."

"I will."

"Tell Winona I say hello."

"I will."

1,071 MILES – OGALLALA, NEBRASKA

Winona II because she looked like Winona. Long neck, thick hips, wandering eyes everyone near her knew could never be satisfied by half-filled silos.

"Her?" Winona II said.

I bet Winona II kept a journal to record her dreams, to speculate about what's out there, spinning the wheel but always landing on: Prince Charming and a view of the ocean from atop a skyscraper. Maybe Winona II wrote about me later, something about the guy sitting nearby that wouldn't/couldn't stop glancing at her, wondering if I was leaving or staying, what role I played in any of this. Maybe Winona still writes about us. I hope she does. I hope there are times that I evolve into Francis on the page.

"Yeah, her." Baby Fat looked at me as if I were intruding so I shoved around my eggs.

Baby Fat because his cheeks still looked like they needed to be stretched a bit. Other than that, he was skinny, some stubble, messy hair. Curious eyes, but not for exploration or ocean air or art school. Just her, Winona II, and it was clear that here was where he hoped he could anchor her heart—in Ogallala.

"Over there?"

"Yeah, she's a dyke." There was no immediate response. "What? It's a word—that's what she is."

Winona II sighed. "What about her?"

"Just look."

Winona II stared at a woman across the restaurant reading a magazine and eating what looked to be a tuna sandwich.

"What do you see?"

"I see the tuna. I see the Cosmo. She's alone. Her hair is done real nice, layered, like she just came from the salon. Cute purse. Coach, maybe. Kate Spade. Am I missing anything?"

Baby Fat shook his head. "You're not seeing it. Switch sides."

When they switched sides I caught a whiff of Winona II's shampoo. She even smelled like her, like that first time we had sex and I was on top and didn't know what to do with my hands so I kept them in her hair and the Melon clung for hours.

"See anything different?"

"Nope."

"Look at her upper lip, at the peach fuzz. You probably think that green tanktop she's wearing is cute—perfect for a hot day, right? The next time she moves, look at her armpits."

"Are there sweat stains?"

"No, the hair."

"That doesn't make her a lesbian."

"Here's the kicker. You'd think that with that tanktop she'd be wearing pants that hug her ass, or a skirt, and some shoes that match, right? She isn't, though. She has baggy carpenter jeans on and she's wearing blue basketball shoes. Fucking Nikes." Baby Fat settled into the booth as if deeming himself victorious. "She's looking at the Cosmo because it's one of the closest things she can get to being a real woman."

I hung my head.

I wish I would've said something to Baby Fat. Winona would, like that one time at Arby's when a punk ass teenager made fun of an old woman struggling to put Horsey sauce on her tray and Winona threw an uncapped cup of ketchup that splattered on the flat bill of Punk Ass's hat. Winona's actions and the old woman's "Thank you" spoke much louder than Punk Ass's "Fuck you, bitch" and exit.

"All right, I'm out," Winona II said. She forced Baby Fat to move so she could grab her purse and light jacket.

"What? Why?"

"Good luck," Winona II said. She stayed by the table for a second before taking off toward the door. "Good luck, with everything. I mean it."

Baby Fat eventually sat back down at the table, his curious eyes unsatisfied with the certainty of what his greasy coffee cup reflected back under the dim light: a distorted boy, alone.

1,460 MILES – RIFLE, COLORADO

Jake called me earlier and said Winona put more pictures of her and Francis online. Without me asking, he said they were taken at some concert and both of them were dripping with sweat, like in that dream I told him about a while ago where I see Winona getting railed by some dude on a beach that can throw her around in a way she likes. A way that scrawny me couldn't. The one that ends with her struggling for breath, fingernails hidden in what specks of fat the dude has on his back, her knuckles white.

"You were right," Jake said. "He is a big guy."

Then he told me they'd miss me at the car wash and he was pissed he'd have to work with dipshit Arthur all summer. I faked a laugh and told him I wasn't sorry. Then he asked if I'd told Winona I was coming. I told him no, that it's a surprise and that it could change things. He called me an idiot and said it wasn't going to change a goddamn thing and to come home so I hung up.

1,733 MILES – AURORA, UTAH

Lots of chatter in the restaurant, which made me think of Coney, of Dad and where he could be now, of Stevenson High School's cafeteria, of Mom watching Ellen, then Maury, then Montel.

"Royce Crosaci, you ginger fuck."

"Bronco."

They shook hands next to their table. Bronco reminded me of a fat Patrick Bateman, slicked hair and three-piece suit rare to Aurora. Royce was a weathered redhead with coffee splatters on his t-shirt from what I took to be a carpal-tunneled wrist.

"How are the kids?"

"Getting to the age where they're out there searching for love."

I wondered at what age I began, when anyone does. I waited for Bronco to tell me there was such a thing to be found in San Diego—the tone in his voice said he knew, the confidence sliding off the back of his tongue, not leaping off the tip—but Royce, Royce needed answers, too.

"I don't know where Becky goes," Royce said moments later, after the coffee came.

"How do you not know?" Again, that slide.

"She told me a while back that she wanted to get a gym membership, but I haven't seen any change in the bank account. She's not paying any sort of fees. I'd see that, right?"

"Does she have her own credit card or something?"

"No. We share everything."

"You sure about that?" Bronco asked. Then: "What does she look like when she gets home?"

"She's still in her office clothes but she, she—" Royce leaned in and whispered the rest, "—she doesn't look like she just got fucked or anything."

I pictured Becky as a woman who was easily ignored in her day to day. Average height, average weight, average stride, average hair, the consequences of such averageness taking its toll when stacked year over year. Not ever truly seen, no matter how many different patterns of pantsuits she'd worn to the office. Not ever truly heard, in meetings, at the water cooler, in her own bedroom, no matter the volume or tone.

"I can't just accuse her of cheating. She'd avoid the question. Flip the situation on its head and make me feel guilty for even considering it."

"You still love her?"

"Of course." Royce's response time couldn't have been gauged by seconds.

"My advice: don't let her out of your sight. Always put a GPS on your bitch. I did. I see where Marie goes at all times now. Home, school, supermarket. Home, school, supermarket. Home, school, supermarket. Get it?"

I pictured this Marie, in retaliation, bringing a world Bronco was ignorant of into their home while he was gone. Banana Republic boxer briefs on the floor, warmed by afternoon sun for the grocery bagger tugging them on before Bronco could open the garage door. Drops of sperm drying on Bronco's edge of the quilt.

I felt my appetite wane.

"Yeah," Royce said. "I get it. You're right. You're probably right."

1,936 MILES – LITTLEFIELD, ARIZONA

Sick of driving. Stopped for the night in another scummy motel. First time I've thought about turning back. Can hear people fucking next door and whoever's on top keeps slapping the walls like it proves a point and I'm afraid to fall asleep because of that beach dream. I don't want to see it anymore, Winona's lips, the flushed knuckles, the wet, tan-lined thighs. She kisses him when she's done, always kisses him not just on the lips, but the forehead. And then they trace each other's interstates on their palms beneath moonlight, waves not crashing like my conscious mind would hope but gently lapping, filling footprints.

1,945 MILES – MESQUITE, NEVADA

He had an Oklahoman drawl when he said, "Willie."

"Trevor."

Willie was a handsome guy—old but fit, with tattoos. He showed me one of a bulldog. Its jaws were no longer fierce but sloppily drooling over his blistered right hand. Mauled by Nevada sun, and age.

"Got that after Basic. Hottest summer of my life. Where you headed?"

"San Diego."

"Boot camp?"

"No."

"Girl then. We do dumb things for love, don't we." Willie phrased this not as a question, but a statement. The correct punctuation. "What's her name?"

"Winona."

"That's pretty." Despite Willie's exterior, pretty was not a hard word for him to say.

"It was."

"Was? Not often a name just up and stops being pretty. What's your story, Trevor?"

"Don't have a story."

"Gonna start one then?"

"I guess."

After that he told me if I loved Winona like he loved his wife to not let her die and I think I was listening because the way the bulldog shivered when Willie spoke of bedpans and IVs and oxygen tanks seemed to wake me up. Those hands, that bulldog could've built many things, destroyed just as much, wandered many bodies. But they were capable of love. And one room, one person had scarred its poor soul still.

0 MILES – MESQUITE, NEVADA

I don't know when I'll see an ocean.

JULIO: CONQUEROR OF THE CROWBAR

2011

JULIO LEANS AGAINST a lamppost yards from where the rest sit, on a bench at the city busy stop. On the bench, beneath an awning, are two women and one man, the latter of whom keeps lifting the left sleeve of his suit jacket and sighing at the dial of his designer watch. As each woman takes their turn staring at Julio, they move their hands as if what's between their fingers isn't a purse strap, but a rosary. Twice now the petite blonde woman has stared and wondered if offering her seat to the child that has elected to stand in the rain would be the decent thing to do. While the heavy woman on the opposite end of the bench has only contemplated it once, of the two, she, ten minutes prior, was the closest to acting upon the thought, struggling to stand and plopping back down once the sound of the bench's relief and the stares of her fellow public transiters forced her face to an anxious shade of red.

Needless to say, for the fifteen minutes they've all been waiting, none of the three adults have spoken to Julio. No one has asked why at 10:30am on a Tuesday, he is here, and not in the back row of Ms. Guiterrez's sixth grade classroom, watching her squiggle the finer details of the Battle of Fredericksburg on the blackboard. He does fidget his hands every so often, as if he has yet to determine where they feel most comfortable: in his pants pockets, or when squeezing the straps of his tattered grey and scarlet backpack. A winter inside has rendered his skin even paler than normal.

"You got that way from your father," his mother has told him before, as recently as Saturday, her Bajío dialect heavy as she broke open the steroid capsules and dumped their powder into the formula already sloshing around the giant metal bowl. "'Go outside for once, northerner, get some sun,' I'd tell him. Light-skinned bastard."

As he has for the past two days—as he tends to do with the few things his mother does say to him—Julio tumbles those words through his skull. Chin to crown, jaw to jaw, they bounce, and lag, like a glitching game of Pong with no goals or paddles, the only endpoint being an interruption such as the approaching bus. Its brakes wince its presence, its approach, its promise of Point A to Point B. The accordion connector wheezes hydraulic pressure into the air.

The man in the suit hurries to the opening door, the two women just steps behind. An automated voice says something a trailing Julio cannot discern. But he walks, eyes, neck, shoulders, everything turned left: a peculiar sidestep rather than a natural gait. His brother's old, soaked shoes squish as he ascends the stairs. He drops in his pocketful of change after the heavy woman does so. Just as he is reaching for the ticket the fare box spits out, the bus driver, a tattooed white man of about fifty, grips his wrist and says:

"Hold up." With his free hand, the driver reaches for the capless Coke bottle from his cup holder and deposits into it one more gob of tobacco spit. He works his dip around his gums and bottom lip, spits once more, then returns his gaze to Julio. "Where you headed?"

"A field trip," Julio says.

"A field trip, huh, all by yourself?" The driver watches Julio nod. "Turn a bit, boy," he says, "no, to the right."

Julio hears a gasp from one of the passengers in the front seat of the bus—either the black woman head-to-toe in white, or from the white girl with caked black lipstick—and understands that it is no use. Despite what they see, none of them will stop this. None will interject. None will rise and unhand Julio from the bus driver.

When Julio does turn, the driver's eyes grow wide at what he sees. Julio's cheek has swollen to double the size of his right; he can open his left eye no wider than a pinky nail; there is a scabbing gash in the center, yellow and purple bruises orbiting. The driver loosens his grip, but does not let go.

"Jesus Christ, kid," he says.

"Can we get this thing moving already?" the man in the suit says from the seat closest to the middle door of the bus, the seat best suited for his imminent leap onto the sidewalk nearest his destination.

The bus driver ignores the man in the suit. He finally lets go of Julio's wrist. "Well," he says, "how'd it happen?" There is a kindness to his voice now, a softness.

And Julio is taken aback by this. He cares not where this kindness is stemming from—whether the driver is a father, a brother, a cousin or uncle—but only that it is there, and that it makes him feel good. Worried for. Needed. It makes him think of his older brother, Oscar, and how, if he were to return home and see Julio's wounds, how the compassionate side of him, once the majority, would ask questions just like this.

"My mother," Julio says, "she hit me in the face with a crowbar."

"Oh," the driver says. The kindness doesn't fade, but it does take on a new shape, evolves from something soft into something lumpy, somewhere between curiosity and knowledge. Like he has seen this before. Like he is conjuring images of Julio being punished for dealing weed, for stealing a quarter pound of sliced ham from the butcher, for spitting in a young lady's hair.

"Drive the fucking bus, would you?" the man in the suit says.

The driver looks back. He grabs his Coke bottle, spits, then swivels into driving position. Before easing the bus into motion, the driver looks at Julio and says, "I guess that'll teach you."

Julio's mother taps the pup's left shoulder with the curved end of the crowbar. The pup—a black and white pitbull with sad cerulean eyes—turns slightly, slacked chain dragging across his already-bulging shoulders, then bites the steel, and cringes before letting go entirely.

"See," Giuseppe says. He stands feet behind Julio's mother, next to Lance, a white man from east of Richmond who'd stopped at an ATM on the way to add to the already-fat wallet resting crooked in his back pocket. He watches the dogs. Over the incessant growling, he strains to hear Giuseppe. Whether or not he hears Giuseppe, whether or not he's on the same page, he nods.

"See," Giuseppe repeats. He straightens his slouch; he folds his arms; he widens his white-sneakered feet; he briefly juts his small, goateed chin: all mannerisms he is certain project confidence. "The steel keeps them in line."

"Wouldn't wood do the same thing?" Lance asks. He watches the pup leap onto his sister's back and gouge her ears with his teeth. She yelps. Together, chains and all, they tumble into the makeshift border between doublewides—satellite dishes, taped together milk jugs, the occasional action figure and plastic fire truck with its hose and ladder snapped off.

"No. No wood. Their jaws become so strong that they bite through. Like kiwi to us." Giuseppe nudges Julio's mother and tells her in Spanish to break the siblings up. It is the first time they've touched in weeks, and Giuseppe couldn't care less. "Watch this," he tells Lance.

Wearing her TACOS HERMANAS work shirt and a pair of knee-high rubber boots, Julio's mother sidesteps through piles of shit and links of chain the pups have already worked off and left to shimmer like gems peeking out of the lawn. Her fake pink nails have been removed, as have the earrings she wore to the market this morning. Yet eyeliner and cover-up remain. A front jean pocket is slightly bulged by her balled hairnet. And she handles the crowbar like a poor, exhausted woman would: with haste, with urgency, shoving the point between the two pups and prying them apart. The boy, having learned moments before that he cannot defeat the object, leaps to his feet. He even backpedals a bit while his sister sees for herself what the steel has to offer. She gnaws on it; she stumbles elsewhere.

"You have to think of the steel as an extension of your arm," Giuseppe tells Lance. "You want them to think—you need them to think—that you are indestructible. That you cannot be fucked with. That you are alpha." Only now does Giuseppe look Lance in the eye. Only now does Giuseppe rub his face with his scarred right hand. Because Lance is no different than the others. A prospective buyer needs to see that the breeder himself is, and has been, a fighter, that he has stabbed and that he has been stabbed, that it's this mentality that will have trickled down to the dogs before him.

But Lance does not look, not for a second. He strokes the entirety of his thick moustache with his index finger. "Can I tell you the truth, Gio?"

"Of course."

Julio's mother walks back to the two men, in the center of her front yard, wishing that, somewhere throughout her nine years in America she'd mastered English. She has tried, several times, and has picked up tidbits here and there—slang, idioms—when she hasn't been seasoning beef and chicken, or mopping floors, or serving hot lunch to charter school misfits. But rules. Hard Ks, Gs that sound like Js, I before E. Rules. Rules. Rules. Too many rules, and too many teachers saying too many different things in too many different tones to navigate. Too many men like Lance chasing more money when they already drive decked-out Silverados down potholed roads and into weed-and-thistle driveways expecting the desperate to not key the tinted windows, or pawn the upgraded exhaust. She wishes she knew English because she doesn't want Lance to fit this projection. She wants the truck to be a façade. She wants him to purchase the last two of this litter. To award

Giuseppe enough money to leave on his own, without confrontation, enough to wander and latch onto the next puta he can trick into giving him her coño. She thinks she wants out of this neighborhood, out of Richmond, out of this doublewide. But that isn't true. She wants out of her skin but has not an idea whom else's she would rather inhabit.

"Well," Lance says. He adjusts the sweat-stained ball cap atop his balding head. "The truth is that none of 'em look like fighters. Not a one. Except for her." Lance points at the pups' mother, who stands erect in the shady corner of the yard, snarling, as she has been doing since Lance's arrival. A thick chain digs into her scarred neck and shoulders. A fly bites at her jagged right ear. "She looks like she could take down a lion."

"She could," Giuseppe says. "As vicious as they come." He puts his right hand on Lance's shoulder. "But she didn't get that way overnight. I can promise you that." Giuseppe, after easing his confident posture into something calm, proceeds to tell Lance what he has been telling men like Lance for a year now, that Lucina, that vicious bitch in the shade saved his wretched life.

###

THE LEGEND OF LUCINA

(paraphrased from Giuseppe's account)

From the moment Lucia and her five siblings were born, to the moment they each were sold, never would she or they drag heavy chains through the lawn. Never would they be deprived of their mother. Never would they attack their siblings' throats over a steroid-sprinkled formula. No. The six played. The six ate. The six pooped. And the six slept. That was all. That was enough. Because Giuseppe's Uncle Fabian didn't raise fighters. He housed dogs. Until they were of age to be without their mother, and could therefore be sold for hundreds of dollars, he showed generations of pit bulls love, and family.

As for what happened to those loved pups after they were sold, Fabian didn't care to know. All sales were final. And not just, "don't contact me if something goes wrong" final, but more like, "I don't ever want to see your face again" final. Anyone that knew of Fabian and his dogs knew the story of Fat Ricky, a neighborhood hustler who'd refused to take Fabian's rules seriously. Weeks after he'd purchased a dog from Fabian, and fought that dog without rest on three separate occasions, Fat Ricky approached

Fabian on foot as he was parking his truck at a gas station and shouted, "You sold me a fucking chump! Nothing but a fucking chump!" The truck had barely stopped moving before Fabian leapt out from the driver's seat and put Fat Ricky—a man who outweighed Fabian by eighty pounds—in a chokehold. Hours later, Fast Ricky would have a bucket of water dumped on his face by the gas station attendant, sit up, and realize that Fabian had stripped him of his clothes and dragged him into the middle of the road.

Why Fabian kept as much distance as he could between what he did with the dogs and what they did with the dogs was simple: he had too weak of a stomach; he was too weepy of a man. From time to time, despite exerting no effort to do so, he'd catch wind of results. Of wins. Of losses. Of wads of cash in cold, ruthless hands. Of bloodied heaps of bone and muscle and heart and love.

Yet, year in, year out, he sold them. It wasn't the only way for a part-time janitor living in a trailer to make ends meet, but it was the only way for a part-time janitor living in a trailer to preserve hope. To put any sort of money away, in an account. To send any money home, to the family members he'd left behind. To have the power to stay, and the power to go.

With Lucina's litter, in particular, by the time buyers came around, poor Lucina had come down with a cold Fabian didn't have the time or know-how to treat. She moved with a lethargy that evoked phrases like, "She won't make it a year," and, "That's all you have to offer?" Nobody wanted her. Nobody wanted her then-narrow shoulders, her then-miniature paws, her then-dry nose and then-exposed ribs.

To Fabian's surprise, at the same time his bitch became pregnant again the health of passed over Lucina rebounded. Because with the trailer, space was always an issue, Lucina became an unannounced gift to his nephew, Giuseppe. He knew that Giuseppe and his girlfriend, Olga, had been fracturing for months. Over jobs, over drink, over the slog life demands. Without something new, without something hopeful, Fabian figured they wouldn't last past winter.

He waited until early one morning when he knew Giuseppe and Olga would be home. And, in the cage she would soon outgrow, Lucina cried for Fabian as he slid back into his station wagon and backed out of the driveway.

"The only chance at reviving the relationship is through common ground," Fabian told Giuseppe over the phone, hours after Lucina was discovered and brought inside. "Through something small, and cute, and in need of love—from both of you."

Lucina continued to cry, off and on for days, when Giuseppe would leave for job interviews and return with not only a bruised ego, but with pocketfuls of rum shooters he used Olga's money to purchase. Only when he would let Lucina out of the cage and onto his chest would the crying stop. She'd lick his face, his fingers, his chin, and, though it in no way made Giuseppe's struggles vanish entirely, it helped. It helped him focus not on what he couldn't do, how he was failing, or what he actually could achieve in this country, but the impact he, if given the chance, could make on the life of something. It helped him remember that legacy doesn't start and end with employment.

It helped up until the moments when Olga—a chesty, trilingual (Spanish, Portuguese, English) secretary for a tobacco farmer named Evans—would come home, walk into the living room, interrogate what she desperately hoped was her soon-to-be groom, and, in discovering the day's (lack of) results, lob harsh, linguistically-tangled slurs his way. To which Giuseppe would sit, and listen, and rub Lucina's soft white ears. The one time Olga slapped Giuseppe during the climax of such a scenario, Lucina nipped Olga's hand. Blood surfaced. And when Olga, her rage transferred to Lucina, reared back for another slap, it was Giuseppe who swatted her hand away.

Later that night, after Olga strayed to another man's hand, Giuseppe brought Lucina into he and Olga's bed and said to her, "I have your back, too."

Within a week, Olga changed the locks and a jobless Giuseppe and a growing Lucina were living with cousins, with old friends, with any other San Salvadorian who'd made their way to Richmond but found themselves in a slightly better situation. They slept on porches, in driveways, and on sofas that had been set on curbs for garbage men to hoist into the backs of their trucks. She lived off of restaurant scraps, and rats she either found hobbled or already dead. He lived off of twenty-five-cent cracker packs, and rum. Their persistence despite the conditions, Giuseppe thought, could only stem from the anger that comes from being unwanted.

One night, on a Main St. bench, when he couldn't take it anymore, Giuseppe held Lucina close and cried into her shoulder. He said no words. He sang no hymn of sorrow. He cried. He sobbed, and she let him.

Another night, Giuseppe, tiptoeing toward blackout drunk, plopped down by a rosebush in Monroe Park and passed out. He still can't recollect what he dreamt of, or how long he actually slept, but he did wake, and when he did, Lucina, standing next to him, was growling. Fierce. Vicious. Tones he'd never heard before. Giuseppe sat up to see the large silhouette of what he'd know moments later, when lying limp, was an eighty-pound German Shepherd. In an instant, without glancing at Giuseppe, Lucina leapt forward and tossed her adolescent paws at the Shepherd's face as if they were fists. The dogs rose on their back legs, a gap between them filled by night sky and dew-covered grass. They growled. They bit.

They danced. And it all made Giuseppe ache. A hundred needles jabbed into his heart.

He rose to his feet as tufts of fur floated to the ground, and increased his pace from a walk to a jog when the Shepherd bit down on the tip of Lucina's left ear. What happened next halted Giuseppe entirely: how instead of letting the pain steer her, Lucina let the Shepherd take the ear. She let the Shepherd tear a chunk of the thing off—a sacrifice for position. She yanked free, cranked her neck, and sunk her teeth into the Shepherd's exposed throat. The Shepherd yelped and Lucina clamped her teeth tighter. She held. And held, until moments later the Shepherd bled out.

"This is my last dime, Uncle," Giuseppe said into the payphone's receiver the next day. "My last one. I need advice, not judgment."

"Advice for this moment, or the next?"

Giuseppe looked at Lucina, fur still bloodied a day after her first kill. Starving. Wounded, but satisfied, and standing tall. "Does it matter?"

Fabian sighed, then said, "Use that dime to feed her. Then, I guess if you're telling me the truth—that

you don't have any other goddamn option—you
fight her."

"Uncle," Giuseppe said, "but it killed me to see
what I saw, to see the teethmarks on her cheeks."
They were deep. It was painful for Lucina to chew.
"I just can't."

"Don't fight her then, what do I care? What do
I know?"

"Uncle, don't be like that."

"Don't be like you," Fabian said. "Use your
head for a second. Just one fucking second.
Understand that you're too stupid to make money
off of yourself. Understand that she's more valuable
than you'll ever be. Understand that she's—" Fabian
continued.

Giuseppe was no longer listening. He was
envisioning what was to come: a day later, Lucina
would win her first official fight. And ten days later
another. Within months, he'd have enough for a
rotation of males.

###

"Now, think of that pedigree," Giuseppe now tells Lance. "You've heard of Makhai? And Segomos?"

"Hers?" Lance asks. "Makhai is hers? Jesus. I watched him rip the jaw off some terrier last month."

Giuseppe turns briefly at the wincing of the city bus's brakes behind him. He watches Julio descend the bus steps with the straps of his faded grey and scarlet backpack over his shoulders, his brother's old, ratty Adidas sneakers looking as if they'll fall apart with any of his next five steps.

"Just think of what these little ones will be able to do for you," Giuseppe says. He points at the pups. "Think of the money they will put in your pocket."

"How do you explain that then?" Lance asks. He watches Julio's mother, crowbar still in hand, scratch Lucina's neck. Her tail doesn't wag, but the growling has stopped. She even lifts her chin ever so slightly, inviting longer strokes.

"Outside of me, she's the only one she'll let touch her," Giuseppe says. As Julio merges from the sidewalk onto the lawn, Giuseppe notices a folded sheet of paper in the boy's hand. With his free hand, Julio waves at Giuseppe, to which Giuseppe nods, surprised but pleased that the boy is intelligent enough to understand an interruption greater than that would be unwelcome at this time. "Let's go inside, Lance, and discuss how you'll be training them."

Lance nods and, with Giuseppe, walks across the lawn and up the two green-carpeted steps leading into the doublewide.

Julio stops feet from the puppies' chained reach and watches his mother stroke Lucina's ears. He wishes he didn't feel a twitch of jealousy whenever he sees this scene beneath the magnolia tree. He remembers leaping with Oscar from root to root. He remembers the two of them failing to clamber up the trunk. He remembers the two of them pounding thick nails on the northwest side so that they would have a route to the lowest-hanging branch, several shelves on which to place their feet.

He still loves that tree. And he still loves this house. He still loves the woman whose name is on the mortgage, but who has allowed everything to slip through her fingers.

Loneliness," Oscar had said so many times, on so many nights, he and Julio up well past midnight, trying within the four walls they shared with one another to figure out why their mother could possibly want to stay with Giuseppe. "There's no other option. Loneliness has to be the driving force. Don't you think, Julio?"

Julio had nodded. Oscar was older, Oscar was smarter. There was no reason to question that what he'd observed had merit. But after a moment, Julio said, "Or fear."

"What do you mean?"

"I don't know."

"No, what do you mean, Julio?"

Julio shrugged his shoulders. "Maybe she's afraid of what he might do if she kicks him out."

Oscar nodded and fell silent, his brow furrowed in thought, as it would be for the two months that followed, until the night he left.

"Hi Mom," Julio says. Lucina growls at Julio's voice so he has to say it again, this time loudly. He speaks to her in Spanish, though, to her constant dismay, the tip of his tongue is not quite as flexible as hers. His mother does not turn, yet he raises the sheet of paper into the air as if she has. "I need you to sign this."

This is a permission slip. What it declares is that, three days from now, on Thursday, Julio and his classmates, supplementary to their recent lessons on the American Civil War, are to board a school bus and travel to Monument Avenue. She will not understand it, and he doesn't need her to. He doesn't need her to know just how interested he is by the conflict, by the battles, by the causes, by the French assistance, the resolutions, or the fact that gallons of grey and blue blood still taint the farmlands. All he needs is her crooked signature.

"What?" Julio's mother asks, still turned. She cannot hear. Lucina's growling grows louder.

Julio raises his voice to repeat himself.

She turns to him briefly, but only to say, "What?" again.

Julio carefully steps closer, looking down so he does not step on the pups, or their chains. This, Julio thinks, this, Julio knows—the failure to communicate—is not the pups' fault. It is not Lucina's fault.

"I need you to sign this," he says for the third time. He takes his eyes off of his feet and looks at his mother, who is turning now, facing him, sidestepping her way back through the puppy shit as Lucina's growling swells. And then there is a sharp pain in Julio's right ankle. Then, the left. The pups are nibbling at him, their sharpest teeth not at all slowed by the fabric of his olive-colored pants. He tells them to stop. He moves his feet. He tells them once more, in English and in Spanish. And then, in one quick motion, he flings the pup from the top of his right foot. He watches the pup land on his shoulder, and is relieved to see him jump to his feet. But, seconds later, Julio is on the ground, holding his cheek. The blood will trickle to his neck when he stands, but not now, not when he is still coming to, when he can only make out his mother's, blurry face, the muffled sounds of his permission slip being shredded by puppy teeth.

###

If there were anything to be learned from the crowbar, Julio feels as if the lesson has been lost, replaced instead by an overwhelming desire to blame. He wants all of the blame to go to his mother. He wants it to rest squarely on her shoulders. But he knows that the placement would be wrong, that, as she has alluded to, at least some of it should go to the shoulders of the father he has met but does not remember. The Seed-Spreader, his mother has referred to him as. The man who stayed put, in the chaos of Mexico City, while his wife packed not only her one allotted suitcase, but the two for their young boys. The man that, no matter where his family was—San Diego, Omaha, Evanston, Richmond—no matter how displaced they felt, no matter how desperate they'd become, never sent so much as a peso.

"He was scared. That coward was scared that all American women are as fat as me," his mother has said before, to both Julio and Oscar. A statement spoken solemnly, regretfully. Infected with shame. "Fat and ugly, stupid women."

But Giuseppe deserves blame too, for the pain still swelling in and on Julio's cheek. He deserves blame for taking Lucina on that walk all those months back, for passing TACOS HERMANAS while Julio's mother, who had bummed a cigarette from Clarita, took a rare smoke break. For letting Lucina approach, and sniff, and somehow, someway, defying Giuseppe's myths, cuddle against the woman's thigh and lick the chicken juice from her knuckles. For persuading his mother to let him move in. For running his operation out of their only yard. For never caring about his mother unless he is rum-drunk. And, more importantly, for driving Oscar out. Poof, in one night, his seventeen-year-old brother gone, to Michigan, to asparagus picking and, "hopefully hay once summer hits," as he's mentioned in the letters he sends to Julio. They arrive once every couple of weeks, usually. Oscar sends them directly to Julio's school, so that neither Giuseppe nor their mother have the chance to read them, or steal the small amounts of cash Oscar bundles within. In one reply, Julio had mentioned that he'd been thinking of their father lately, trying to remember what he looked like. The next envelope from Oscar came within days. Rather than a letter, its contents consisted of a sketched portrait of their father. Bushy eyebrows, slick hair, low cheekbones. SEED-SPREADER! was written beneath the man's strong chin.

Julio has always looked up to Oscar. He's always appreciated Oscar. But, as much as he hates to think of it, he's beginning to understand that he, too, is deserving of blame. He may listen to Julio, he may talk with him and not at him, he may send letters and drawings, but the truth is that Oscar—not their mother, not Giuseppe—made the choice to leave. To abandon. To strip away the only armor his brother has ever known, and shove him into a battle he doesn't know how to fight.

Julio would give anything to receive a letter proving his thoughts wrong. Julio would give anything to tell any of them what he was doing, right now. I skipped school to take my own damn field trip, he'd say, or write. You hear me? All by myself, all for myself.

His face grows hot at the thought.

When two young women wearing matching red, white and blue T-shirts that shout, SAVE OUR UNION, hop onto the bus and raise their voices, Julio welcomes the distraction. They pass out fliers for some protest as the bus continues down the street. They shout that democracy today is a codeword for fascism. Passengers take the fliers, yes, but they return quickly to the urban decay outside of their window, blurred at this speed.

Julio turns his attention to the man splayed on the seat across the aisle. A damp green bandana is stretched from eyebrow to scalp, containing the frizz of his curly blonde hair. He possesses a beard of wizardly proportions, a dark blonde base with the occasional smudges of brown and grey. His eyes are shut. He snores lightly, and when the bus goes over a pothole, or jerks to a stop, the man's khaki combat boots swing. They just swing. Never to life, never to action. Just back and forth. What Julio finds most interesting, however, beyond the aforementioned, beyond the green army jacket, are the bullet casing tattoos stretching from knuckle to nail on each finger of his limp left hand. Within each casing are numbers, or letters, something rendered illegible either by Mother Nature or Father Time. But, even if they don't anymore, even if they have lost their luster, they once stood for something. They are a nod. An ode. A symbol. They, Julio thinks, once made a monument of his flesh.

Julio, standing in the center of Monument Avenue and Lombardy Avenue, gawks at a bronze J.E.B. Stuart. Stuart's saber is drawn. The horse he sits atop is rearing, readying for movement, following the order to take charge, to sprint toward and, eventually, through wave after wave of blue-coated men and cannonballs.

Julio is not joined by his classmates, or by anyone, really, the only passersby being a trio of tourists with heavy cameras strapped around their necks. The only thing, then, that throws Julio out of his stare, out of his desire to hop the fence and climb Stuart's granite pedestal, out of his desire to sit atop that horse and look down on Monument Avenue— its brick mansions, its elaborate churches—is the traffic. It is noon. Hungry Richmond workers honk at their inability to speed through a red light. Those at a stop gawk not at Stuart, but at Julio, at what he is convinced is his embarrassingly swollen cheek.

It's enough to make Julio move, to ignore the crosswalk and beeline through halted traffic to the sidewalk, and up the street, northwest, past large brick buildings, some with skinny chimneys at rest, others punctuated by pillars, until the sidewalk veers further north, beginning the traffic circle in which Robert E. Lee has been erected.

Including the pedestal, Lee and his horse are sixty feet above the grass beneath them. Lying on the lawn, enduring the mist, are what appear to be college students. Some toss around a football. Others close textbooks and opt to chat, sliding their pencils behind their ears. Leaning on the fence surrounding Lee are three people in raincoats, none of whom, as Julio can't help but doing as he proceeds northwest, stare at the tiered granite hoisting the statue and wonder if the tiers are meant to resemble steps. Steps that lead to Lee. Steps that lead to that rusting door beneath the statue, to Lee's heart, to Lee's soul. Because Lee, Julio thinks, is open. Lee is accommodating. And, though Julio someday soon wants to accept that invitation, now is not the time. He must heal before he does so.

He walks on, up the sidewalk, watching panting huskies and terriers brave the humidity and chase Frisbees across the grassy median. Of course, he thinks of Lucina, and wonders just how wrong Giuseppe has treated her, if any of his words can be taken as truth, if she really took down that Shepherd, or if those scars on his hand are actually from alley-way brawls over booze or women. For a moment, Julio pictures himself leashing Lucina and bringing her here, not to fight, not to squabble over a territory she has just claimed, but just to walk, to wade amongst the normal.

Just then, Julio feels it. He feels it, and then he sees it: a red-haired woman staring at him, at the wounds on his face. Julio squeezes his fingers around the backpack's straps. Sidesteps. Seeks space—

—which he finds it beneath Jefferson Davis. Davis, he has learned from Ms. Guiterrez, served as president of the Confederacy and, for this reason alone, he finds his monument to be fittingly extravagant—Davis himself, when compared to the entirety of the sculpture, is small, rendered nearly insubstantial by the size of the columns half-surrounding him. But Davis, as if recognizing that he alone weren't strong enough independently, has his right arm lifted and his hand open. "Rise, rise," it says to Julio. "Join." But join what? Julio wonders. THE ARMY OF THE CONFEDERATE STATES, as the inscription on the left-most column says? THE NAVY OF THE CONFEDERATE STATES? Join in numbers? Or, join the woman Davis seems to be lifting his arm toward—Miss Confederacy perched atop the Doric column in the center? Julio doesn't have an answer. But he walks, up the steps, back down, then around the monument, on the right side. He grazes his fingers over the Latin phrase he does not understand, but reads aloud, PRO ARIS ET FOCI, before the approaching family of three are parallel, their conversation a series of whispers. The family stares. Julio returns to squeezing his backpack straps. He sidesteps until there is distance between them.

Julio walks past the heavily-trafficked statue of Stonewall Jackson, and thinks nothing else but that Jackson, other than facing a different direction, looks like he is mimicking Lee. Atop a horse. Proud. Staring down traffic. Eyes down, Julio moves past, moves forward, maneuvers around the crowd standing before the statue of Matthew Fontaine Maury, past the bronze earth and sea that weighs so heavily on the man's head. Off Julio goes, away from all, legs churning.

What causes him to stop, what completely and utterly confuses Julio, who had been led to believe that Monument Avenue was and is a place to commemorate those who stood up to what they thought was tyranny, is what he finds when he walks upon the Monument and Roseneath intersection. Because there, twelve feet tall, stands Arthur Ashe. Gazed upon by no one. He has seen the name before, on street signs, but he does not know who Arthur Ashe is, what he has accomplished. But he is black. And he looks angry. Angry, in a wrinkled tracksuit and rimmed glasses. The marble children standing beneath him appear to be excited, anxious even, for the tennis racquet Ashe is about to hit them with, or the books he is about to drop on their heads. Not a saber, Julio thinks. Books, and a tennis racket. Not a uniform; a tracksuit, and glasses.

###

"Julio," Oscar says. His hand is on Julio's shoulder, shaking him awake. "Julio, get up."

Julio rises and groggily looks at Oscar, at the clock, and across the room. It is 1:14am. His brother's bed is made. Not a pillow or blanket missing, or in disarray. And Oscar, Oscar is in jeans, a blue jacket and orange stocking cap. On his back is a bulging black backpack. In his eyes is a look of certainty, of conviction, that what he is about to say, that what he is about to do, is pure, absolute, and moral. It's this look that keeps Julio—who looks so young on this night, his hair much longer than what it will be on Monument Avenue, his own eyes just wet, fluttering blobs of miscomprehension—silent, eager to listen.

"I need your help," Oscar says. As far back as Julio can remember, Oscar, reliant on the self, has never uttered these words. Not to him, not to anyone. But those eyes. Once more, those eyes. Unblinking. Like stone. "I'm leaving, Julio, and I need your help."

"Okay," Julio says.

He gets out of bed, slips on a t-shirt and a pair of pajama pants and awaits instruction. Which he doesn't verbally receive. Oscar nods, then leads Julio out of their bedroom and alongside a sleeping Giuseppe on the living room sofa, stomach-down, face buried into the throw pillow. An empty pint of rum rests on the floor, flanked by an empty twenty-ounce Coke bottle. The way Oscar stares at Giuseppe as he and Julio pass says that what Oscar really wants to do is climb atop Giuseppe's back, grab handfuls of that curly black hair and bury his face into the pillow even further. He doesn't want a fight; he wants a kill. There's a rage in those eyes that Oscar is and has been struggling to contain. But he has: since the first night Giuseppe stayed; when he and Julio first heard their mother's headboard clapping against the wall, he has; he has since Giuseppe pulled them both aside one Saturday morning weeks after and said, "I'll be staying here some nights and you need to respect that."

The night Giuseppe moved in permanently, Oscar paced around he and Julio's bedroom. His hands were in his hair: "I don't want that drunk fucker here, Julio. I don't. I don't want his dog here, I don't want him on our couch, I don't want him eating our food. I don't want him in our mother's bed."

To which Julio replied, "Have you told Mom?"

"At least ten times. And you want to know what she says?" Oscar sat on Julio's bed then. "She said that I'm a burden. Said that she'd be primping herself up in some three-story hacienda if it weren't for me. Said Giuseppe would take her there. That I have no say."

Julio watched his brother shake his head and mumble something into his palms before asking, "Did she say that about me too?"

"No," Oscar said quickly. Too quickly. His eyes sold him out. Lies. How many had he told Julio over the years? He brought his hands back to his face. Spoke into them: "Of course not, Julio."

And now Oscar is sliding those same hands beneath their mother's mattress. He squats and, backpack still on, quietly pulls the mattress off of its box spring, off of its frame. Only then does he employ Julio's help, positioning him at the foot end of the mattress while he circles toward the headboard.

"What are you doing?" Julio whispers.

"Just lift," Oscar says.

"No." Julio won't. "Not until I know."

"I'm going to burn it," Oscar says. "And then I'm going to leave."

"Why? Why are you leaving?"

"You know why. And, once I make enough money, I'll help you leave, too." Oscar lifts his end of the mattress. "Now, will you help me or not?"

Most of Julio doesn't want to. He wants to let Oscar do this all on his own. He wants no part in the destruction, in the chaos, not when Julio will have to deal with the consequences of their actions entirely on his own, with Oscar long gone. He does not want to declare war; he wants to go back to bed. He doesn't want to leave. He wants to be in Richmond, in what throughout the past three years has become something of a home. He likes his school. He likes Ms. Guiterrez. He doesn't want to move again. Doesn't want another Omaha. Doesn't want another Evanston. He doesn't want another environment to shove him back into his shell, to kill the lights and lock the door. Because here, in Richmond, he can feel that shell starting to peel away. He knows street names. He knows which buses will take him where. He is certain that this city can play a part in the story of himself.

"What if he wakes up?"

"He won't. He's drunk."

Julio looks at the digital clock on his mother's nightstand. "She's going to be home soon," he tells Oscar. And she will, after the last-call wanderers of Richmond have been fed. She'll walk in with sore feet and hands, stinking of TACOS HERMANAS chicken, makeup smeared, dark blue shirt damp with sweat.

Oscar still holds the mattress in his hands. "That's the point." He sighs. "Julio, please, just help, or get out of the way."

Moments later—after they, without so much as a nudged coaster or lamp, maneuver the mattress out of the bedroom, around Giuseppe and what will soon become his couch, through the front door and to the gravel driveway— Julio, though he wouldn't know how to explain it if asked, feels the fear wash away and something new take its place. He feels both sad and oddly satisfied. His stomach is full, his heart heavy. He feels with Oscar, not for Oscar. He, too, feels as if he is stepping eerily close to independence, to success, to accomplishment. It's pride. That's what he feels. Pride.

"Thank you," Oscar says to Julio in the driveway. He walks to Julio and gives him a hug. He even kisses his kid brother on the forehead. "I'll get you out of here. I promise. I will."

Julio nods. He wonders if he should cry here, in this moment. Because he doesn't feel the urge to. The hug was too brief to be final. Oscar will be back, he thinks. Oscar just needs a break. He'll be back soon. He will.

"Get inside," Oscar says. "You tell her that I did this. Hear me? You had nothing to do with it. Understand?"

Julio does. He says so. He nods. And then, as instructed, he goes inside, directly to what has in just one moment become solely his room. He opens the blinds. He watches Oscar douse the mattress with lighter fluid, then drop a lit match. In a moment, once he's deemed the fire before him satisfactory, Oscar will be gone, down the sidewalk and into darkness, reduced in Julio's life to this moment, to the handwritten letters that will follow. And, soon after, with the mattress still smoldering, his mother will park on the street and look around the neighborhood. She won't touch the mattress. But she'll shout. Oh yes, she'll shout, and she'll storm into the trailer, and Julio, still watching it all from his dark bedroom will jump into bed. He'll pull the covers over his face. He'll listen to her and Giuseppe yell. He'll hide. And he'll stay hidden like this for the months to come.

###

The rain has stopped. Brief as it was, the sun came out, but is now tucking itself beneath the quilt of night. With what light remains, Julio, looking down at the driveway, is convinced that he can still spot where the mattress turned to ash, where the flame blackened the gravel. But his eyes are deceiving him. Just as there are no cars in the driveway, there is no trace of the defiant moment that redefined Oscar. Outside of the squealing tires of a neighbor gunning his rusted Trans Am through an oft-ignored stop sign, the only sound is Lucina's growling. She cannot see Julio from the magnolia tree but she knows he is here. And she's known all along what he is capable of.

Julio walks to the edge of the doublewide and looks toward her. The pups are gone. Not one tumbles about, not one gnaws on a stick. Gone. To their new homes, their new lives. To cages. Julio grips his backpack straps and slouches while Lucina, despite the weight of the chain around her neck, stands erect beneath the magnolia, alert. Julio says nothing. Does not growl, like her, does not bark, does nothing but turn, walk across the lawn, up the two steps and into the house.

He walks through the living room—past the Giuseppe-stained sofa, past the empty bottles that have accumulated atop and beside the coffee table—to his bedroom. Days after Oscar burned her mattress, Julio's mother took it upon herself to drag the two twin-sized mattresses out of Julio's room and into her room, leaving Julio with only box springs. And this has gone unchanged, as has the placement of the box springs, Julio never having seen the point in stacking them, or rearranging them to maximize floor space, not when he's been sleeping on a pile of blankets, not when Oscar's return is inevitable. But, since yesterday, since the crowbar, since this afternoon, since Monument Avenue, since Arthur Ashe, that perceived inevitability is fading in Julio's mind. So much so that he flings his backpack at his brother's box spring. The backpack rolls to a halt while Julio is slinking to the floor. He touches his left cheek and grimaces, absorbs the pain. Runs his hand through his hair and listens to Lucina's chain scraping the magnolia's trunk.

And there is just too much, far too much colliding in Julio's brain. Oscar, his father, Giuseppe, the bus driver, Stonewall Jackson, Jefferson Davis quarreling, dancing, twisting, melding to one another, into something sharp, something much sharper than that crowbar. It is that sharp point that continues to puncture the good memories Julio has of his mother. The way she carried him up, down and across the streets of San Diego. The way she would smother his, and only his Omaha steaks with garlic butter before pan-frying them. How, in Evanston, she had Julio read his thin books to her before bed. How empowered that made him feel. How important. But they're oozing. The memories are oozing, binding, solidifying until Julio can find a semblance of the clarity he seeks. Two options, he thinks. There are two options, he knows, has known, will always know. Run, or—

The yellow beam of the old flashlight bobs as Julio walks quickly across the yard. Lucina rises, approaches, barks, lowers the barking to a growl, stretches her chain taut. Julio slows. He sets the flashlight on the grass so that Lucina's mismatched ears are swathed in yellow.

Julio, planted just feet outside of her reach, inches the curved end of the crowbar toward her. She sniffs the metal; her ears droop, from angry to anxious; she retreats. Julio advances. Steps his calves into the yellow light, then his knees and thighs.

He stares at Lucina and grows sad at the way her eyes are now shifting from the grass to the crowbar, from the crowbar to him. His eyes water. He begins to rethink what he has come out here to do, what he has for an hour now been considering. He ponders dropping the crowbar, stuffing his backpack with underwear and socks, with non-perishable food, and hitting the road, finding his way to

Michigan. Leaving what he wants to become home without so much as a wave. Conceding.

"I'm sorry," Julio says. He can't. He won't. This is where he will stay. "I'm sorry," he says again, and wraps his free hand onto the crowbar, gripping it now as if it were a baseball bat.

Lucina cowers.

Julio swings.

Lucina cries, barks, bites.

Julio swings. Again. And again. And again, growling his way through the sounds of the crowbar connecting with Lucina's stomach, through the cries, through the cracking of ribs, through the physical surrender of what he knows is not his enemy.

Julio swings until Lucina is on her side. Blood has not yet reached air. She does not cry; she does not bark. Her tongue is on the grass. Her paws twitch.

Only when Julio catches his breath does he start sobbing. He buries his face into his shirt sleeve as he approaches her. He crouches. Pets her neck.

"I'm sorry," he says. "I'm sorry. I'm so sorry."

Moments later, Julio stands. He wipes his eyes, then regrips the crowbar. Rotates it in his hands so the pointed end is against Lucina's fur. Julio's hands are shaking.

"I'm so sorry," Julio sobs. "I'm so sorry."

Julio leans his weight onto the metal. The crowbar pierces Lucina's skin. Strikes bone, until it is redirected by Julio's pre-adolescent hands and shoved through the other side of Lucina, until Giuseppe's trophy has been anchored to the ground.

He lets go of the crowbar. Backs his way out of the yellow light. Studies what he has done. This is how he will leave her. He wonders if this is how they'll all remember him, in the dark, leaning against the magnolia tree.

MEN OF ACTION

A BOY WATCHES a television program with his mother where the camera follows an elderly lady in a beige pantsuit as she interviews impoverished women on sidewalks. One of the three interviewees screams at Jesus over a husband whose amputated toes were fed by mob hands through a Midtown sewer grate. Another sobs for a tire-ironed brother limp beneath the entrance of a parking garage. The last, a junkie with dime-sized sores on her cheeks, chirps her gratitude when the lady in beige hands her a pair of thick yellow socks for the upcoming winter.

"My husband will love these," the junkie says, holding the socks high.

In his ten years, the boy has not seen his mother cry. But there, on the opposite end of the sofa, she wipes her eyes. There are tears near her collarbone, this same woman who commanded a megaphone in front of thousands at the last neighborhood march, this same woman who as a young girl refused sleep for days after out-jogging ground zero debris.

Are you okay? the boy asks.

Yes, the boy's mother says. Women can cry happy tears, you know?

###

The boy walks like a heron toward his mother's salon. His red stocking cap compresses his shaggy hair, his jug-handle ears. The alleys, he has been warned since the television program, are off limits. He is to never go up them, or down, or across, no matter the time and energy they'd save. But he has been here before, has listened, has walked this sidewalk, thousands of times, has sidestepped passersby, has seen these buildings, has felt small in their shadows. Most days he stymies his curiosity by keeping his eyes on his breath, silver swirls in the cold. But it's warmer today. His breath has no outline and he has no muse. The boy's eyes wander, from brick to brick, from skyscraper to sky.

He passes an alley. A barback tosses days old finger foods at the beaks of five or six pigeons. The boy approaches another, in which two whiskered men wearing faded parkas fight in slush over a torn scarf. The smaller man's chin, the boy sees, is bloodied. And a tooth—yes, a tooth, the boy confirms—is lodged between the larger man's thumb and index finger. Blood smears to his wrist.

The boy stops. He watches for a moment. And another. He listens, to the grunts, the scuffs, the slurs, the curses.

Hey, the boy says. He says it meekly, quieter than a mouse.

Oblivious to the boy, the whiskered men just tussle, and tussle, and tussle, leaning, heaving, bending as one. When all is over, when the larger one lies unconscious, face shattered, the victor will walk to where alley meets sidewalk and find no boy, but an offering. Into his front pocket the red stocking cap will go. And the boy will in that moment be sprinting, to the embrace of something he'll fear losing for some time, but deep down knows he's already lost.

Q&A

09/05/1995

CM: I know you're just trying to help, but you need to be careful. Addison, do you hear me? Please be careful when you step on and off the stool. Okay?

AM: Okay.

CM: Thank you.

AM: Is that how Grandpa fell?

CM: Here, hand me that bowl. Now give me the towel. See how I wipe the entire thing down—the bottom, the edges? We can't put wet dishes in Grandma's cupboards.

Remember? Here, you try. That's better.

AM: Mommy?

CM: Yes, Addison?

AM: Did you want Grandpa to die?

CM: What? No. Nobody wanted Grandpa to die. You hear me? Nobody.

AM: Then why did Grandpa die?

CM: We all die eventually, sweet pea. Some people get sick. Some people die from accidents. Some die just from old age.

AM: Why?

CM: Because we can't live forever.

AM: Why can't we live forever?

CM: Because we just can't. It's not how it works; it's not how we work. That hasn't stopped people from trying, though.

AM: What do you mean?

CM: People have been trying to figure out how to live forever for years. They build things, they tinker with new medicines—

AM: Tinker?

CM: It means to play with. To explore.

AM: Explore?

CM: Yeah, sweetie, explore.

AM: What do they explore?

CM: Lots of things. Diets, exercise, pills, treatments.

AM: But they haven't figured out how to live forever yet?

CM: Addison, come on, what did I just say a minute ago?

AM: Be careful stepping on the stool.

CM: Yes. Thank you. But not yet, no, people haven't figured it out. Maybe when you're all grown up they'll have it so you can just eat a piece of chocolate and live forever.

AM: I'd like that.

CM: You would, would you?

AM: Yeah. I don't like death.

CM: What don't you like about it, sweetie?

AM: It's scary.

CM: It is. I know it is. Do you wish that Grandpa could've lived forever?

AM: Yeah.

CM: I understand.

AM: I wish he wouldn't have died because then Grandma wouldn't have made me cry.

CM: How did Grandma make you cry?

AM: She cried in the church, and she wouldn't stop crying, and I cried at her crying.

CM: It's never easy to see those we love in tears.

AM: I love Grandma.

CM: I do too, sweet pea.

AM: Did you love Grandpa?

CM: Here, just set that heavy dish on the table. We'll take care of that one later.

AM: Mommy?

CM: Yes, honey?

AM: Did you love Grandpa?

CM: There were times that—well, did you love him?

AM: I didn't like it when he was mean to Grandma.

CM: He wasn't very nice to your daddy either.

AM: His voice was scary when he yelled.

CM: Yes, it was. We all yell, though. Daddy yells. I yell. Even you yell.

AM: I yell?

CM: Of course you yell, silly.

AM: Wyatt yells.

CM: Wyatt yells pretty loud, doesn't he?

AM: Mmhm.

CM: And you love Wyatt, right?

AM: Yes. I love Wyatt very much.

CM: I know you do. And that's what I think I'm trying to get at somehow. People do things that make us sad, that make us mad, they say things they don't mean, but we—well, we just keep on loving them, don't we?

AM: Does Daddy make you mad?

CM: Your daddy makes me mad all the time.

AM: All the time?

CM: All the time.

AM: But you still love him, no matter what?

CM: No matter what. I mean, how many times a day do you see me kiss your daddy?

AM: Once in the morning, once before bed, and as many times as you can between.

CM: And can you remember why do we do that, Addison?

AM: I don't remember.

CM: Oh come on, yes you do. In the hospital, before Grandpa went to sleep, what did Grandma say to you? When she sat you on her lap, what did she say?

AM: Kisses con—kisses con—.

CM: Kisses conquer all. That's right. They help us forget the yelling. They help us forget the crying. Grandma says it all the time: kisses conquer all. And now she said that to you, didn't she?

AM: Yeah.

CM: Listen, sweet pea: we kiss those we love as often as we can because we just don't know how much longer we have with them. Do you understand?

AM: I understand.

CM: Good. Good, good.

01/18/2000

CM: Mrs. Price—

KP: Ms. Price.

CM: Ms. Price, I don't think we're quite understanding you. Is she kissing her desk? Her book? Her locker? A plunger? What?

KP: No, Mrs. Myers. I'm afraid Addison has been kissing each and every boy and girl in her class. She gives out kisses while the students are hanging their coats. She gives out kisses during recess, as well as at the end of the day, before the students walk to their buses. She has even tried giving kisses out to Mr. Borming, while he has attempted to diffuse the situation time and time again.

CM: Jesus.

KP: As you can imagine, there have been some complaints. Parents have called Principal Eaves and have begun to question the ways in which the school is run.

HM: Which parents?

KP: That isn't relevant, Mr. Myers.

HM: I think wanting to know who has a problem with my daughter is relevant.

KP: Let me rephrase, then: I can't give out that information. Even if I could, I wouldn't. Because the other parents and their phone calls are not the issue here.

HM: But my daughter is an issue?

KP: I'm not saying Addison is an issue, sir. But her behavior most definitely is.

CM: Has she said anything? I mean, does she say anything about why she's kissing?

KP: She has. But sense has yet to be entirely made from her responses. Which is why you're here—details need to be gleaned; gaps need to be filled. Mr. Borming, who has witnessed this issue first hand, and who has asked Addison on multiple occasions about her behavior, believes that Addison is a frightened child.

HM: Frightened? Of what?

KP: That she's going to lose her classmates, Mr. Myers. When Mr. Borming has asked her why she feels the need to kiss her classmates, she has replied on multiple occasions with something along the lines of not knowing if she'll see any of them tomorrow. Has she said anything of the sort to either of you at home?

HM: No—

CM: Yes—

HM: When? When has she said something like that?

CM: I don't know. But she has, Hud. To me. To Wyatt.

HM: Well, I've never heard it.

KP: And you didn't see that as a problem, Mrs. Myers?

HM: She's ten years old. Kids her age say things they don't mean all the time.

CM: How long has this been going on, Ms. Price?

KP: It's been happening for about seven weeks now.

CM: Seven weeks?

KP: Maybe even longer. The first reported incident occurred sometime during the second week of December. While you wouldn't be wrong in wanting either myself or my colleagues to contact you immediately, Mr. Myers is right in saying that overreaction isn't the best approach. That said, we'd decided to let it play out, acting under the assumption that what had occurred, and what continued to occur, was a phase, perhaps even a product of the Y2K scare. We thought maybe she was just acting out of fear, that, coupled with what she explained her reasoning to be, she'd simply seen too much on the news. But, as you know, Y2K came and went. The kissing continued. Here we are.

CM: Okay. Okay. Okay, so what comes next? What do we do? She gets to stay in school, doesn't she?

KP: In no way do we intend to remove Addison from school. Please don't worry about that. All we'd like you to do today is answer a few questions. From there, we all can decide how best to go about this.

HM: Now just wait a minute. I understand what you're saying. Really, I do. I understand how this can be viewed as an issue. But, do you honestly think our daughter—that girl out in the hall, slumped against a locker, thinking she's started the apocalypse—is doing something so wrong here? Maybe I'm missing something, but is kissing really that bad? Would you rather have her sit at her desk and do nothing? Say nothing? Feel nothing?

KP: Try and think of this from my point of view, Mr. Myers, from another parent's point of view. Imagine your daughter being ill—carrying something contagious—and continuing this behavior. I can only assume you've heard of mononucleosis. Meningitis? Imagine several children contracting that illness. Are we to shut the school down then, because of a kiss? Spread of illness is only the first tier of this issue. I mean, if something of that magnitude were to happen, it isn't like Addison would be the one and only culprit. It's a school. Illness walks in and out of here every day. The second tier of this issue, however, the one I'd be most concerned about, is what would happen if we were to let this just run its course without interruption. A year goes by: she's still kissing boys and girls. Fine. But three years from now, four years from now, once she's menstruating, what then? Beyond the cruelty of the words she'd hear, what if the kissing advanced to other activities, with several partners? You're talking about sexually transmitted diseases, you're talking about pregnancy…I have plenty of statistics to offer, if that'll help support what I'm saying to you.

HM: No thanks, Ms. Price, you've said enough. And you've wasted enough of my time. I'll see you at home, Caroline.

CM: Hud, where are you going?

HM: Plenty of streets that need plowing before dark, don't you think?

— :

CM: I'm sorry about that, Ms. Price.

KP: It's quite all right, Caroline. Can I call you that?

CM: Of course.

KP: If you'd prefer, we can hold off on the questions until the next time your husband is present. Or, we can proceed as outlined. I promise, the questions won't take much of your time.

CM: Sure. Sure, we can go ahead. I'll just catch him up later. I'm really sorry he acted like that though. Truly.

KP: It's okay, Caroline. It's normal for strong feelings to arise from protector types; they feel threatened by the issue with their child; they feel like they've failed. But, let's get started. My first question is: Has there been a death in the family recently?

CM: Not recently. No, the most recent one was five years—

yeah, about five years ago now—Hudson's father died.

KP: I'm sorry to hear that. How'd he go?

CM: He'd had a long battle with prostate cancer.

KP: Was Addison close with him?

CM: I wouldn't say she was close, no. She saw him, sure, she

knew most of what was going on. But close? No, I wouldn't

say that.

KP: What about Wyatt?

CM: He was closer to him than Addison was, definitely.

KP: And what kind of a relationship do Wyatt and Addison

share?

03/03/2003

WM: She's being a little slut.

CM: Watch your mouth!

WM: Those aren't 'my' words.

HM: Then why the hell would you say them? Think that's

any way to talk about your sister?

WM: You don't see her every day, Dad, not like I do.

HM: You're right. I don't. But if I did, I can promise you I wouldn't call her a slut. Look what you did to your mother.

CM: I'm fine.

WM: Mom, I didn't mean it. Really. It's just, well, didn't we get this taken care of?

HM: Told you therapy wasn't worth a damn.

CM: Dr. Monaghan says that she's improving, that she's starting to open up.

WM: I'm not trying to be insensitive, but I don't think I'd call her taking random dudes into bathrooms and kissing them an improvement.

HM: At least it's just dudes now. That's a plus, isn't it, having that part figured out?

CM: Hud, stop it.

HM: What? I find that to be a relief, Caroline.

WM: I'd rather they be girls, honestly. There'd be a lot less bragging and high-fiving.

CM: Stop. It doesn't matter what you'd prefer. It doesn't matter what either of you would prefer. Wyatt, be honest— she just chooses random boys and drags them into the bathroom? You've seen that happen?

WM: I haven't seen it, no. But I hear it, Mom. I hear all about it. If I don't hear it from Rick or Jordy, it's from some freshman whose friend just cut class and walked over to the middle school.

HM: Wait, Rick and Jordy are—

WM: Jesus, Dad, no. They hear things and pass them on to me. Listen to what I'm saying. Please?

CM: So they're approaching her now?

WM: The freshmen? Why wouldn't they? Freshmen are desperate.

HM: I'd say. To walk that far—

CM: Dammit Hudson, I'd really appreciate it if you took this seriously. It's not something to be blown off.

HM: You want me to be serious?

CM: I think that now would be a better time than any to be serious.

HM: Fine. I'll be serious. Wyatt, you know who these guys are, right?

WM: Most of them.

HM: Then beat the shit out of them. They talk about her like that? Punch them in the nose. They make that walk to the middle school? You leave class straight away and punch them in the nose.

CM: You're unbelievable.

HM: You asked for serious. This is as serious as I get.

WM: You really think that's going to help, Dad?

HM: I do, yes. Addison's reputation isn't going to change, so you change the narrative with your action. Word gets around that those in pursuit of Addison have an obstacle, they'll slow their pursuit.

CM: What about the discipline that's sure to come from that? Wyatt turns into the enforcer, patrols the schools with his fists. Addison slows down, but Wyatt doesn't go to college—because Wyatt goes to jail, because Wyatt's tethered to the house. Meanwhile, Addison's alone at school, and we're worse than we were at square one.

HM: I'm not saying Wyatt keeps the act up day after day. I'm saying that he punches a couple of them, off school grounds, preferably, and it's going to make a big difference.

WM: I'm not punching anyone, Dad.

CM: I'm all ears for whenever you have another 'serious' suggestion.

WM: But what about me?

HM: What about you?

WM: I'm tired of hearing about this shit.

CM: Language.

WM: Every day, I get made fun of for her being my sister. Every day, some new smiling jackass walks up to me and says how he can't wait to bone Addison.

HM: They say things like that?

WM: Yes. They do.

HM: What are their names?

WM: Their names don't matter, Dad.

HM: Why am I the only one that thinks it matters that someone tells them they can't say that about someone? Why am I the only one who thinks bad behavior should be corrected by those that have the means to correct it?

CM: Because it isn't that simple, Hud. There are repercussions to everything.

WM: I'm still not hearing any suggestions on what I should do.

CM: What about me?

WM: Huh?

CM: What about me, Wyatt? You don't think I deal with parents all day? You don't think that they come into Mandrell's and look at me like I'm telling Addison to do all of this? That I'm behind all of this? Of course they don't say anything about it. No, they keep it professional, ask me to explain their current policy, inquire about the next step. But they know exactly who I am. They know who my daughter is.

HM: You know that extension of the courthouse we're helping build? People have been driving by, and walking by, and they've been waving, but they stare, too. Make sure it's who they think it is. Lean over to their kid or spouse and tell them whose father I am. Walking into the courthouse itself is worse. Much worse. All that small talk, always tiptoeing. I hate it. Every second of it.

WM: So we're obviously all affected by this. What do we do then? Home school?

CM: And have me or your father quit our jobs? We can't afford that.

HM: What if we send her away?

CM: Send her where?

HM: I don't know. Idaho, Colorado.

CM: Boarding school?

HM: Why not?

CM: I don't think opting out of the problem and forcing someone else to solve it is the best route.

WM: Isn't that essentially what you're doing with her therapy?

CM: Look, I just don't think a different zip code would solve the problem.

HM: Well, what else is there?

WM: Lock her in her room. Tell her she's Sleeping Beauty or something.

CM: Brilliant plan, Wyatt.

WM: I don't hear you suggesting anything.

CM: What if we just stay the course? Have her keep going to therapy, let that do its thing. Deal with the comments, the looks. We stay patient, we lean on one another, we stay—

AM: I'll stop.

—:

HM: Hey sweetheart.

WM: How long have you been listening?

AM: I said I'd stop, didn't I? I do what you want. Isn't that how this is supposed to work?

CM: Sweet pea, you don't—sweet pea, don't cry, come here.

11/10/2004

QR: Little cold for a walk, isn't it?

AM: What?

QR: I said, it's a little cold for a walk, isn't it?

AM: I'm fine.

QR: Tell that to your cheeks and nose.

—:

QR: I'm Quentin, by the way.

AM: I know who you are.

QR: Come on, hop in.

AM: I'm fine, thanks.

QR: Your brother would kick my ass if I just drove off.

AM: He should kick his own ass then.

QR: He left you here?

—:

QR: Why?

AM: Such a mystery.

QR: Come on, I'll take you home. Either I take you home, or I drive alongside you the whole way.

AM: Prepare yourself for a slow go of it then.

QR: At least let me cut a couple miles off for you. Call it hitchhiking. I need to stop for gas anyway.

AM: Should I stick out my thumb to make it more real?

QR: If it'll make you feel better.

—:

AM: It smells like feet in here.

QR: Sorry. Conditioning started Monday.

AM: Wyatt wanted to try out this year.

QR: Why didn't he?

AM: Could be that he sucks at basketball. Could be that my dad told him to get a job. Could have something to do with me. I don't know. Never said.

QR: Oh.

AM: Yeah. Oh.

QR: Did I say something wrong?

AM: Wrong? No. Oh's just the worst possible thing to say.

QR: Okay. No more, 'oh'. Does that mean tonight you—

AM: Go ahead.

QR: Go ahead what?

AM: Ask me who. That's everyone's first question: who? As if that's all that matters, who-who-who.

QR: Look around. We live in a town of, what, 2,000 people? What you do, and who you do it with, it's going to be talked about. 'Who' does matter. To some, it really is all that matters.

AM: That's why I can't wait to get out of this damn place.

QR: You're thirteen years old.

AM: Fourteen.

QR: Okay, fourteen.

AM: And that means I can't want something?

QR: That isn't what I said. Look, you wanting to get out of here is normal. I do too. But I'm seventeen. I'm gone before summer hits.

AM: So?

QR: What I'm saying is that you should probably try as hard as you can to get that thought out of your head. The next couple of years are going to eat you up if you don't.

AM: Where are you heading off to?

QR: Oregon. Salem, Oregon.

AM: What college?

QR: To hell with college. Overpriced. Worthless to me. My dad lives in Salem. He's one of those guides for when you want to go hiking, or kayaking, or whatever.

AM: Is that what you want to do, you know, for your job?

QR: Maybe. I don't know. I'm trying to manage expectations, but I thought I'd at least get a taste and see what I think. My dad said falling into it was one of the best things that happened to him. I have to get out and pump; you staying here?

AM: I'll get out.

— :

QR: Does Wyatt know what he's going to do yet, when he's done?

AM: He wouldn't tell me if he knew.

QR: I sit near him in chemistry. All he does is doodle. Thought maybe he was hoping for an art school or something.

AM: What does my asshole brother doodle?

QR: Just shapes, I think.

AM: Oh.

QR: Pretty quiet kid.

AM: Didn't used to be that way.

QR: What happened?

AM: Me.

— *:*

QR: If you were so accepting of it all, if you believed in what you were doing, I don't think you'd be so down on yourself. So why do it then? Is it some kind of disease?

AM: A disease?

QR: Disease, condition, whatever.

AM: I don't think so. I don't know. Maybe. But it's what people expect of me now. Guys just come to me, won't take no for an answer, not from the girl that made out with Carl Treehorn, or the girl that gave Vance Barnes a handjob. 'What do those douche bags have that I don't?' they say, 'Why them and not me?' So, I make them happy. Because isn't that what you're supposed to do? Do things to make others happy? Isn't that what we're told our purpose is?

QR: You really gave Barnes a handjob?

AM: Yeah. Why?

QR: Barnes?

AM: Yes, fucking Barnes. So what? You want me to tell you how big of a dick he has? You want to know how fast he blew it?

QR: No, no. I'm just surprised is all.

AM: At what?

QR: Most girls aren't so open about something like that.

AM: Yeah, well.

QR: Going inside to pay. You thirsty or anything?

AM: I'm fine.

QR: Okay. But I think you're wrong.

AM: About what?

QR: I don't think making others happy should come at the expense of yourself, or others, for that matter.

AM: It always does, though. Make one person happy, you make another sad. By hurting someone, you help someone else. Give and take.

QR: Whatever you say. You sure you don't want anything?

AM: I'm fine.

— :

QR: Can't beat two for two bucks. Which one do you want?

AM: Dr. Pepper.

QR: You still live on South Thompson?

AM: Yeah.

QR: Want me to drop you off somewhere nearby? Let you walk the rest of the way, show Wyatt how tough you are?

AM: I don't need to prove anything.

QR: Front door it is.

AM: Quentin?

QR: What?

AM: How many girls have you kissed?

QR: How many?

AM: Yeah. How many?

QR: Why do you want to know?

AM: Maybe I want to know how weird I really am. Or maybe it's that I want to feel normal. Tell me.

QR: One.

AM: One?

QR: Yeah, one.

AM: Just one?

QR: Yeah, just one. Is there a problem with that? How weird does that make you feel? Does that make you feel normal? Jesus.

AM: I feel no different.

QR: Well?

AM: Well what?

QR: Aren't you even going to ask who it was?

AM: I told you, the who doesn't matter.

QR: It does to me. The who is supposed to mean something.

AM: Who was it then?

QR: Chelsea Geist.

AM: She's pretty. Like, model pretty.

QR: She is.

AM: Did you like her?

QR: I loved her. That's why I kissed her.

AM: Do you still love her?

QR: Some days I do. Other days not so much.

AM: When she's dangling herself over Brent?

QR: Yeah.

AM: They're inseparable.

QR: I know.

AM: But let's back up a bit. If I kissed you right now, would it mean that I love you?

QR: What? That's not what I said. That's not what I said at all.

AM: Yes, it is. You just said that love drives a kiss. So why can't a kiss drive love? Can't kissing make people feel loved to the point that it can make an awful day stop on a dime?

QR: That's quite a thought for someone your age.

AM: Years of being fed over and over what people are 'supposed' to do has a way of making you think for yourself. Just answer my question, Quentin.

QR: Which one?

AM: Can't kissing make people feel loved?

QR: I guess, yeah, but—

AM: But what? You can't just go around kissing strangers? Yeah, I've heard. But why not? Ask anyone I've ever kissed, they'll remember that day. Surprised? Sure, some were. But angry? Disappointed? Not for a second.

QR: I think that you'd feel differently if you'd ever been in love. You'd know that a kiss has more value than you're giving it now. That it's more sacred. You'd know that a kiss is a reflection of that feeling and it happens because the moment has been built up to the point that you don't know what else to say, that you don't know what else to do with your hands, or your eyes or your lips.

— :

QR: Have you ever felt that?

— :

QR: That's it ahead, right?

AM: Yeah. Yellow mailbox. Here's fine though.

QR: Here you are, Addison.

AM: I would say thank you, but I didn't ask for any of this.

— :

QR: Aren't you going to get out?

AM: I don't want to.

QR: What do you want to do then?

AM: Talk. I want to keep talking with you about love.

DA: Mrs. Myers, I'm Detective Andrews and this is Detective Trestman, how are you this afternoon?

CM: Hello.

DA: We came here today to share some new information on the whereabouts of your daughter, a Ms. Addison Myers. Can we come in?

CM: Sure, sure. Of course. Have a seat.

DT: You have a very lovely home, Mrs. Myers.

CM: Thank you, Detective—Trestman, was it?

DT: That's right, ma'am.

CM: Would either of you like some coffee? I just made a pot. Or juice?

DA: Coffee, please. Black will be just fine.

DT: Same here. Thank you, ma'am.

DA: I understand you're the only one home today, Mrs. Myers.

CM: Yes, it's just me. My husband and my son stepped out for a bit.

DT: Do you have any idea as to where they went?

CM: They didn't say. They just said they were heading out.

— :

DA: Mmm, now that's some good coffee.

DT: Yes, very good. Thank you, ma'am.

CM: You said you have some new information on Addison?

DA: We do. But first, I wanted to let you know that, as we speak, Hudson and Wyatt are being escorted back to the house here.

CM: Escorted?

DT: Yes ma'am. It's more of a precaution than anything else.

DA: I'm sure Officer Thomas informed you that, since the night of Addison's disappearance, we've had eyes on your house for any unusual activity. So, naturally, when Hudson and Wyatt loaded shotguns into separate vehicles and took off at the exact same time, we had patrol cars ready to tail.

DT: While we understand the frustration all of you must feel, it wouldn't be helpful for our investigation if they were to take the law into their own hands.

CM: I understand.

DT: To let you know, in case he brings it home with him, your husband wasn't especially happy about our apprehension of he and Wyatt. But Wyatt understood right away.

DA: He seems like a good kid.

CM: He is.

DT: He was supposed to bring Addison home from school that day, wasn't he?

CM: Yes. Yes, he was.

DA: And he didn't because he was upset with her?

CM: Yes, that's correct. He feels horrible about it now b—

DA: Guilt's quite a natural thing in this scenario, Mrs. Myers. It's likely to subside after we find Addison, though.

DT: And we will find her. We're all working very hard on that. These things happen more often than you'd think, ma'am, which means we're all the more capable of getting your daughter back, and quickly.

CM: Officer Thomas mentioned that. Technology, he said, leaps and bounds.

DA: That's correct. And it's served us well so far in your daughter's case.

CM: What do you mean?

DT: Ma'am, what do you know about Quentin Reede?

CM: Quentin Reede? The name sounds familiar. I want to say that he's in Wyatt's class but I'm not sure.

DA: Yes, yes he is.

CM: What about him? Do you think he's the one that took her?

DT: We've been led to believe that, yes, your daughter is with Mr. Reede.

DA: We've had an Officer Barrow maintain a close eye on the attendance records at Bottineau High School and, it turns out, Mr. Reede is the only student other than Addison who has been absent each school day since her disappearance.

DT: All seven of 'em.

DA: Which is a substantial amount, especially when, after questioning his mother—a Gabrielle Tedesky, remarried— we discovered that not only had Quentin not been showing any signs of illness, she, more importantly, hadn't seen him for over a week.

DT: We asked her whether or not she found that odd—odd enough to notify someone—to which she replied more or less that she just thought he'd been staying with a friend.

DA: Her ignorance, while perplexing, didn't appear to be an attempt to cover anything up.

CM: So Addison's with Quentin?

DT: We can't say that with absolute certainty, at least not yet.

DA: But it is a lead, a strong lead, which is more than we've had so far.

CM: But why? What the hell would Quentin Reede want with my daughter?

DT: Well, ma'am, you said it yourself that your daughter was a bit, uh, how do I say it, promiscuous

CM: Yes. I don't know if that's the word I used, but—

DA: It's only a matter of time before a predator pounces on that type of behavior, Mrs. Myers.

CM: Does Quentin have a record of doing that? Are we talking about sexual assault here?

DT: No, ma'am. I mean, we can't rule such a thing out but, as for Quentin's record, it's clean. One speeding ticket, one parking ticket.

DA: Which understandably makes all of this a bit foggier than one would expect, as there doesn't seem to be a clear motive.

DT: For all we know, Addison asked him to take her.

DA: It isn't a stretch of the imagination to say so, considering her past.

DT: What Detective Trestman actually means is that kids do these things, ma'am. Sometimes without reason. Or, if there is reason, of any sort, they can't even put it into words. The important thing, though, is that we get her back here.

CM: When do you think that will be?

DA: Sooner rather than later, Mrs. Myers.

DT: Mrs. Tedesky was rather helpful in telling us that a few months back Quentin's father gave Quentin a credit card of his to use, you know, in case of emergency. We've been tracing that card.

DA: The last purchase made here in Bottineau was at the Shell station downtown. Gasoline, one Dr. Pepper and one Diet Pepsi. The next purchase made with the credit card was at a Wal-Mart in Williston. Two pillows, two blankets. Then, breakfast at Denny's in Miles City, Montana. A few more minor things after that—

DT: The last stop we have on record is in Bend, Oregon. Gasoline.

CM: Oregon?

DA: The boy's father lives in Salem. We believe that's where they're headed.

DT: Do you have any family in Oregon? Any friends? Any reason for Addison to go along with this?

CM: No. I've never even been to Oregon.

DA: Has Hudson?

CM: No, not that I know of.

DT: What about Wyatt?

CM: No. Never. Salem, Oregon?

DT: Yes ma'am.

CM: Is that where they're going to be taken into custody?

DA: In addition to calling the boy's father, we've alerted the Salem Police Department, as well as every other law enforcement agency in that area. We've faxed them photographs, statements, what have you.

DT: Needless to say, that's where we anticipate they'll be apprehended. From there, they'll be transported back to Bottineau and we'll proceed accordingly.

CM: Quentin Reede? Salem, Oregon?

DT: I know this is probably a lot to take in. I mean, we know how rough this can be on a mother as caring as you. Just try to stay as positive as you can, and please do call us if you need anything, anything at all. Okay?

CM: Okay. I'll do that, Detective Trestman.

DA: You ready there, Paul?

DT: Thank you very much for the coffee, ma'am.

CM: No, thank you. You don't know how much of a relief this is, to actually have an idea.

DT: There will certainly be more to come, ma'am. Take care now.

CM: Wait. Detectives?

DA: Yes, Mrs. Myers?

CM: Once they're taken into custody, can you please give me a call? I'd just like to know all that I can before I see my daughter.

DA: Of course. What we hear, you'll hear.

FLASK

I KNOW I'M NOT supposed to touch niggers but Mrs. Graham's fingernails are teal and Mom's fingernails were teal the day we buried her and I touched them a lot that day. Her hands were real cold and steady. It was nice. Dad said he thought it was nice too.

Dad is waving at me now. He doesn't like me standing by the dead body. He never has. Mr. Xavier is by Dad and he starts waving at me too. I don't know Mr. Xavier that well but I like his name because not many words that start with X sound like a Z. He's nice to me though and when I walk over to them, Mr. Xavier pats my head like I'm a dog and says, Hey Lukewarm. Then he says something to Dad about putting too much of a big word I don't know how to spell and another big word I don't know how to spell in Mrs. Graham and laughs. Mrs. Graham does look more swollen than dead bodies usually do. Dad doesn't say anything but he laughs and pulls his small silver bottle from his suit and takes his 31st sip of the day.

Since Mom died Dad takes more sips. Before she died he would take nine or ten sips and he would be really silly. He'd lift Mom up and twirl her in the living room and he'd tell me knock-knock jokes. Knock knock. Who's there? Mustache. Mustache who? I mustache you a question, but I'll shave it for later. That was his favorite. I'd laugh and he'd laugh and Mom would laugh. He let me take a sip once when we were driving home from Grandma and Grandpa's. I didn't like it because it burned my throat and it made me dizzy for just a second. I told Dad I didn't like whatever was inside and I asked him why he did. He said it was because it made him calm when everything was busy. But Dad says Mr. Xavier and him are always busy because people don't stop dying, which is true. Which might be why he takes at least thirty sips a day now and isn't very silly anymore.

Dad has been really busy since Mr. Xavier called Dad and told him they were going to start putting those big words I don't know how to spell into niggers. I thought it would make Dad angry because since Mom died he's been telling people that niggers took her nerves. But Dad just shook his head, shrugged his shoulders and told Mr. Xavier, We'll just charge the coons more then.

I don't know how much Mom cost but the wake was nice and I remember people I didn't even know telling Dad, I'm so sorry for your loss, and Dad saying back that we'll miss her more every day, which still confuses me. Am I going to miss her even more than I already do? Does thinking about her hands shaking count as missing her? Am I supposed to be keeping track of how many times I think of her every day? Miss Cawl saw that I wrote those questions on my sheet of paper one day when I was supposed to be writing something else. I was scared about what she might say but she said those were good questions to ask. Then she told me to put the questions away and start on my work. I like Miss Cawl.

Just then dad and Mr. Xavier stand up straighter because Mr. Graham walks to the front of the room and asks everyone to be seated. The room quiets down and sits. Dad takes his 32nd sip. Mr. Graham tries to talk but he doesn't get very far before he starts crying. They look like really heavy tears. I think his kids are up front because the oldest girl stands by Mr. Graham and says, We all loved my mom in some way or another and while it's a shame she's gone we know God has a plan for all of us. I raise my hand so I can ask her what God's plan is for me and if God has talked to

Mom but Dad puts my arm down. He tells me to be quiet and to listen.

###

I'm eating by myself in the lunch room. People usually don't sit by me and that's okay. Being alone lets me think of things I wouldn't think of if I had people talking to me all the time. I keep thinking of the writing assignment Miss Cawl had us do this morning. I can picture the paper. I can remember word-for-word what I wrote.

Lucas Carlson
14 May 1962

Mother's Day

Mother's Day is Sunday, but Mom won't be there, because Mom died 113 days ago. Mom was very nice to me, and was a good mom. When I had a bad day at school, she would tickle my armpits until we both started laughing. I miss that.

She was a good cook. I really liked when she made Hot Dogs, because they would be crunchy and soft at the same time. Dad just gives them to me cold. Sometimes he tries to make things Mom used to make, but they aren't as good. I tell him it's good, but he knows it isn't so he doesn't eat much anymore.

I miss walking home from school, because Mom would meet me at Doc's General Store and walk with me the rest of the way and ask me how my day went. Now I go to Grandma and Grandpa's house most days after school, and it's not as fun, but I love them because they're Grandma and Grandpa.

I miss skipping stones with Mom at the creek, because when we would come home Dad would laugh at how wet our pants and shoes were. Dad even came once or twice, and he would skip them the farthest, and he would skip them up the creek instead of across and let the current catch the stone and make it stop. I think he might want to just stop again because he's always so busy.

Dad doesn't say he misses Mom, but I know he does because

That's when time was up so I hurried to put the commas where they were supposed to go. I really do miss skipping stones though. It was usually just me and Mom and she'd say, You're so good at it Lukie! and it would make me smile. She wasn't very good at it because of her hands but she'd always tell me how I good I was at using my eyes and to just keep those eyes up. And we would stop for ice cream at LaBelle's on the way home, even in January. But that was the month she died so I don't think I'll get ice cream in January anymore.

I take a bite of my sandwich and look around the lunch room. Gerry Langford is in line behind Josie Meekourt. Josie's the prettiest girl in school and she smells like dandelions. I think Gerry is too busy shoving kids to like dandelions. Gerry shoves the same boys around every day until a grown up gets angry and yells. Then he stops and everyone seems fine. It makes me think I have to get angry for someone to listen. But I'm not good at being angry. Maybe I'm good at being sad because it makes me sad that since Mom died Gerry doesn't push me around like he pushes the other boys.

After lunch, I go to class. And after school, I go to Grandma and Grandpa's. When I get there, Grandma asks if I think we can finish the puzzle we've been working on for 34 days. I tell her, I don't think so but we can try, and she smiles and puts a piece in the bottom right corner, which completes a building next to the church that takes up most of the puzzle. Grandma says the church is in New York City and that she's been there once and that it's one of the prettiest things she has ever seen. She says, If God isn't in that church I have no idea where he is. I ask her if she thinks that's where God does all of his planning and she laughs and says, Maybe.

Grandpa walks into the kitchen and asks how I'm doing. Grandpa's a lot bigger than Grandma in every way but his voice is just as high, which seems strange to me because Dad and Mr. Xavier have really deep voices. I tell him, I'm good, and he says, Good, and gets himself some potato chips and walks out of the kitchen. After Mom died Grandpa wouldn't come out of the bedroom and see me when I came over. I've never asked why but I think it's because Grandpa told me once that I look a lot like Audrey and he didn't want to see her anymore. Mom did say that her and Grandpa didn't always see things the same way.

Dad picks me up around 6:00. The car smells stale and sour at the same time and I ask Dad, What's making that smell? He says, I don't smell anything, but I still do so I roll down my window. Dad says, I'll show you where it smells bad, and rolls his window down to smoke. I don't like the smell of smoke either so I put my nose close to my window.

We drive the opposite direction of home and outside there are some white kids playing. Girls in dresses chase one another around a yard while boys that are a few years older than me throw a baseball back and forth. Dad says this is a good neighborhood. I agree because I see dads sitting on their decks and drinking and moms sitting in their yards trying to catch the sun, which is something Mom used to say.

As Dad passes Jackson's Pharmacy, he says that this is where it gets bad, but I don't know what he means. It's quiet like the other one and kids are playing in yards like the other one and in parks. Next to Jackson's is Fred's, which is a restaurant I've never been to. It smells really good. It smells like the food stand at the fair. I ask Dad why he thinks this is such a bad neighborhood and he says, It's too dark here. I tell him, The sun is still out. He says, The sun can't make niggers any lighter. We drive past Fred's and I see a nigger boy about my size and with hair as orange as mine being pushed around by two boys bigger than Gerry Langford. It really doesn't seem that bad to me.

I guess Dad and I aren't going to church. I woke up at 7:30 because Mom always woke up at 7:30 on Sundays. I waited until 8:00 to wake Dad up but when I tried he started talking in his sleep and I couldn't understand what he said.

The room smelled like Dad spilled at least 22 sips on his sheets.

I think about going to church by myself but I don't think Dad would be happy to wake up and see me gone. I don't think he'll be happy when he wakes up and church is over either. I'm confused about what I should do. So I go back to my room and get dressed. I don't know how to tie ties so I wait for Dad to wake up because it won't take him very long to tie my tie for me. He doesn't wake up until 9:45 though and when he does I'm sitting on the stairs. He walks past me and says, Good morning Lukewarm, and I say it back but I don't think it's a good morning because we missed church and I wonder if God will have a new plan for both of us now. I say, We missed church, and Dad just nods.

The phone rings. Dad answers it and I listen from the stairs. Dad says that he's sorry and then takes a long pause and says that he knows everybody's wondering about him and me and more so now that we didn't go to church and he says he's sorry again but it doesn't sound like he means it and he says, Goodbye, and hangs up. I go into the kitchen and ask, Who was that? Dad cracks some eggs and says it was Grandma.

The phone rings again while we're eating. Dad sighs and tells me to answer it. Mr. Xavier is on the other end and says, Hey Lukewarm, and asks for Dad. I tell Dad it's Mr. Xavier. Dad shakes his head then picks up the phone and says, Yeah? I walk back to the dining room and hear Dad say, Another nigger? Then he says, Jesus Christ. Mom wouldn't like him saying that. Then I think Mr. Xavier makes a joke because Dad laughs and says, Can you handle it for now though? I wait for Dad to hang up before I ask what Mr. Xavier wanted. Dad says, Nothing, then asks how the eggs taste. I say, Good, but I don't like that I did because Mom wouldn't like me lying like that.

When Dad gets out of the shower he comes into the living room. He smells a lot better now. He sits next to me on the sofa with the Sunday paper that Johnny Winston threw at our door this morning. Dad likes to look at the sports section. He always gives me the obituaries page because he says he knows who died already. In today's obituaries are Thomas J. Ketchen, Sally Marigold Bosnick, Lois Deborah Thorpe, Orwell Thurston Podge, Brian Jefferson Waldrip, Audrey F. Trinks. I stop there for a second because I always do when I see the name Audrey. It makes me think about Mom's obituary that I cut out and put in a box I keep under my bed:

Audrey Christine Carlson

(2 September 1931 - 26 January 1962)

Audrey Christine Carlson, 30, of Ozark, went home to be with the Lord Thursday January 26, 1962. She was a loving wife, proud and devoted mother, and all one could ask for in a daughter. The family is grateful for the support they've received in this time of need.

Audrey was born Sept. 2, 1931 to Mitchell A. Rysmith and Eleanor (Denison) Rysmith. Audrey graduated from Sterling County High School in 1949, where she soon after met her husband, Walter Carlson of Tuscaloosa, AL.

Walter and Audrey were married March 21, 1951 in Ozark. Audrey worked at Nails and Such Salon as a manicurist until she became pregnant with her son, Lucas.

She is survived by her husband, Walter; her son, Lucas; her parents, Mitchell and Eleanor Rysmith; sister, Doris (Rysmith) Engles of Tallahassee, FL. She was preceded in death by her grandparents, Alfred and Betsy Rysmith, her father-in-law Reginald Milo Carlson, her mother-in-law Mildred Frances Carlson, and her brother, John, who was taken too early by disease as well.

Audrey will be remembered for being the spark of her family, for having the spirit of the Lord and for passing that on to her husband and son. She will be greatly missed by all.

I remember Grandma kept tissues on the table when she wrote it. Dad was quiet but kept nodding when Grandpa read what Grandma wrote. After Grandpa finished reading he looked at Dad and said, You really don't have to prepare her. Dad just asked if teal was okay. Grandma and Grandpa smiled. Then Dad left for Mr. Xavier's and Grandpa went to the bedroom.

Dad turns the radio to a baseball game and puts the sports section on the floor. He takes sips but I don't know what numbers yet. I keep looking over the obituaries because I can't find Mrs. Graham. I couldn't find her last week either. I ask Dad why I can't find Mrs. Graham and he says it's because the paper doesn't print anything about the death of a nigger. I tell him, That's mean, and he asks why and I say, Because niggers should be included, and he says, Sure. I ask Dad if he has a wake tomorrow and he says, Yes. I tell him I want to go. He asks me why and I say, Because I like Mr. Xavier's, but it's really because I want to hear the family talk about God's plan again. I want to know what it means. I would ask Dad but I don't think he'll want to talk about it, especially if he doesn't want to go to church anymore. He'd just tell me to ask Grandma or Grandpa and I don't want to do that either. I don't want Grandpa to go back to the bedroom and I don't want Grandma to cry. I hate seeing her cry.

I don't want you at any more wakes, Dad says. End of story, he says. I tell him, I'm not a baby. He says he knows and asks if I want to go play catch instead of argue. I say, Sure, and I'm excited because we haven't played catch in 242 days.

In the yard Dad waves at people driving by and honking their horns. I remember one time I asked Dad, Why do so many people know you? And I remember him saying, Because every living person knows someone who died, which makes sense. Ready Lukewarm? Dad asks now and I say, I'm ready, and he throws the ball really high so that I lose it in the sun. But I catch it. I catch it because 297 days ago I begged Dad to show me how to handle a fly ball. I toss the ball back and tell him to throw it faster. He says, OK, and he throws it faster. I catch it and he says, That's great Lukewarm, and I toss him back the ball as fast as I can. Dad misses the ball. He's breathing heavier than I've ever heard him breathe and he's sweating more than I've ever seen him sweat. He picks up the ball. I say, Throw it faster, and he throws it faster. I catch it again and it hurts my hand. I toss the ball back but Dad misses the ball again. He starts walking toward the ball but then all of a sudden he stops and takes his glove off and throws it at the house. Then he grabs the ball and throws that at the house too and it makes a huge Thwack when it hits the door. Between deep breaths he says, I'm going to sleep, and walks inside.

Grandma asks me to help her with her flowers and I say I will. Grandpa says he'll help too. As soon as we go outside Grandma starts pulling weeds in the flower bed. For being so old she can bend over really far. Grandpa walks over to me and says, She's flexible huh? Grandma says to stop it but she laughs and he laughs and I laugh too but I don't know what I'm laughing at.

Grandpa asks Grandma where she wants all the flowers that are sitting in pots on the lawn. Grandma says she'll decide in a minute. Grandpa sits down on the grass and it looks like going from standing to sitting hurts him. He hurt his shoulder before I was born. I don't know how it happened but I can see it on his face that it still bothers him.

I sit next to him and look at the clouds. One of them looks like a cat with its tail curled and I point that out to Grandpa. Grandpa agrees and points out another one and says it looks like a whale. I don't think it looks like a whale but I don't tell him that. I ask, What kind of whale? He says, Blue, and I nod because it's the only kind of whale I've ever heard of. Neither of us talk for a few seconds but I wish I had more to say to him.

After the clouds pass over, Grandpa picks a flower from one of the pots and hands it to me. He tells me to smell it. I think it smells like Mom but I know not to tell him it smells like Audrey. I tell him I like it. He says he's always liked those flowers. He tells me they're called hy-a-cinth. I ask him why he likes them so much and he says that his mom had them around their house when he was a kid. It's hard for me to picture Grandpa as a kid. His hair now is silver so I don't know what color his hair could've been then or if his nose was any smaller. Mom always told me I had Grandpa's nose but I don't think our noses look alike at all.

I ask Grandpa if we could put some hy-a-cinth-s around Mom's grave and he says, There are already some there. Grandma tosses an orange flower on the grass and says, We can take that one to Audrey's grave. I say, What about that yellow one? Grandma gives me that one too.

After we have a bunch of colors Grandpa asks me if I miss Mom and I say I do and he rubs my head and says, I miss her a lot too.

Dad pulls into the driveway. He walks real slow and his eyes are shiny but have big bags weighing them down. Dad looks at the flowers and says they look good. Grandpa says, Lukie here did most of the work, and I laugh and say, No I didn't. Dad looks at me and says, It looks good. I tell Dad we're going to take a bunch of flowers to Mom's grave. He doesn't smile or anything but he says, That's good. Then Grandpa asks Dad if he's doing OK and Dad says, I'm doing just fine.

We stayed inside for gym class and threw footballs to each other because it was raining. Gerry Langford was my partner but he wasn't trying very hard and threw the balls up high and soft. I caught every one of them and told him to throw the ball faster but he never did. I started dropping the balls on purpose because I thought maybe Gerry would get mad at me and push me or throw them faster. But he just kept telling me I was doing a good job. Then he made fun of Garrett Billings for dropping so many balls next to us and it had me really sad and I don't like that Gerry Langford makes me sad.

I'm not so sad when the sun comes out but it makes me think about going to the creek after school instead of Grandma and Grandpa's. Even though it's been 151 days since the last time I skipped stones, I don't think Grandpa would want to go because it would hurt his shoulder. And Grandma's not really into that kind of thing because she likes puzzles and flowers. I don't know who else to ask because the only other person that talks to me is Miss Cawl and all she says now is, Good job, when she hands me my work. But that's all. This morning she just set my Mother's Day writing on my desk and said, Lucas, and moved on to other kids after looking at me like I was supposed to say I was sorry for something.

The bell rings and Miss Cawl reminds us of the math homework for tonight that I started at lunch. I walk behind Josie Meekourt on the way out of school. Because she likes dandelions so much I thought she'd notice the yellow shirt I wore today. But she didn't. She still smells really good so I can't be mad at her. She walks to the buses in front of the school, which is the way I'm supposed to go to Grandma and Grandpa's. But I stop and let other kids walk past me. I don't want to go to Grandma and Grandpa's today. I think about going to the creek again but I know I can't do that by myself. The only place other than Grandma and Grandpa's I can go is to Mr. Xavier's.

###

I walk into Mr. Xavier's and there are niggers in black everywhere. Some are seated and some are standing but they're all looking at me. I think it's because of the yellow shirt. All the stares makes me nervous. But none of them stare for very long because there are a bunch of nigger kids younger than me running around and laughing, which is better than crying. At Mom's wake there were a lot of young kids that didn't know how to act either and their parents let them run around because they were too busy talking to Dad or Grandma and Grandpa and crying.

I wait at the front for Dad but he never comes so I walk to the casket. It's really small. When I look inside I see a nigger boy about my size and in a black suit that's too big. His skin doesn't look like it's about to burst like Mrs. Graham's did. I look closer. His hands are together over his belly and his tie is around his neck and his orange hair looks red under the light and I can see a smear from a kiss on his

145

right cheek. His eyes are shut really tight and so are his lips. I want to touch him but I know I'm not supposed to.

After the clouds pass over, Grandpa picks a flower from one of the pots and hands it to me. He tells me to smell it. I think it smells like Mom but I know not to tell him it smells like Audrey.

Just then someone asks me who I am and I turn around to see it's a boy that looks exactly like the boy in the casket. Exactly like him! The only difference is that his eyes are open. I tell him, I'm Lucas Carlson, and he says his name is Carlton Smiths. I say my last name and his first name are almost exactly the same but he doesn't laugh or smile like I do. He tells me he's never seen me before. I say I haven't seen him either. I say, I don't see many niggers with orange hair. Carlton pushes me in the shoulder and says, Don't call me that. I say, I'm sorry, and I really am because I didn't know. I think of all the times Dad has said that word and I wonder if he knows he isn't supposed to say it. He asks if I knew his brother and I say, No I didn't. He says they were twins and I say, That's strange, because I've never seen twins before. He tells me it was nice having a twin because sometimes they would even dress alike on their aunt's birthday and would play tricks on her and their uncle and their cousins. I say, That would be funny.

Carlton tells me he feels weird that everybody is sad and I tell him that everybody is supposed to be sad. He says, Really? I say, I know because Mom died 118 days ago. Carlton asks, How did she die? I say, Her hands kept shaking and her legs quit working. Carlton says he's sorry to hear that and I say, I'm sorry about your brother. Carlton points to his brother's hands and says, He was stabbed. I say, Stabbed? Carlton says, With a knife. I don't know why anyone would want to stab Carlton's twin. I ask, Was it someone like me? Carlton says, They were white but they were older than you, and I say, Good, because if it were someone like me I would feel really bad. But then I feel bad for saying good and I say, I'm sorry. Just then an older dark woman says, Carlton! Get over here! Carlton says it was nice to meet me and I say, It was nice to meet you, and Carlton walks over to the older dark woman.

I feel a tug on my backpack. I almost fall over. It's Dad and his breath smells like he just took his 40th sip. He says, What the hell are you doing here? I don't want to make him angrier so I tell him the truth. I say, I didn't feel like going to Grandma and Grandpa's. He squats down and says, You can't be here. I ask him, Why not? He says that this is no place for a young boy alive or dead. I tell him that I've been here before and that I can behave. He says, That doesn't matter, and tells me to go to his office and to do my homework.

Dad takes me up to the office and calls Grandma and tells her that I'm at Mr. Xavier's. He sounds really frustrated and tells me to stay put. Before I can tell him I will, he slams the door shut. I do stay put for a while but there's a window up here so between math problems I walk to the window and look outside at the parking lot. Eventually all the people come outside and I spot Carlton walking to a car with the woman that called him over earlier. I try to open the window but I can't figure out the locks. So I tap on the window and hope that Carlton sees me but he doesn't. The rest of the people down there look up instead. Dad is out there too and looks up and shakes his head. I watch him walk inside and I can hear him jog up the stairs. I sit back down at the desk and act like I'm busy.

###

Miss Cawl told us to write about friends today.

Lucas Carlson
21 May 1962

I made a new friend yesterday. His name is Carlton. I met him at Mr. Xavier's because that's where Dad works. I met Carlton while I was looking at his twin brother who was stabbed. I never learned his dead twin's name because Dad made me go to his office. But I know they were twins because Carlton said so. I think I met Carlton because I've been looking for a friend and maybe it's God's plan that he made up in a church in New York City.

Dad wasn't happy that I went to Mr. Xavier's after school because I was supposed to go to Grandma and Grandpa's but I didn't want to. I'm glad I didn't because me and Carlton are friends now. But I don't know if Dad will like that because I think Dad will just say he's a dark boy and I can't be friends with him. I hope that's not true because Carlton was really nice.

###

I can't tell if Miss Cawl liked My New Friend or not because all the paper said when she gave it back was to see her at lunch today. She's never asked me to eat lunch with her before. So at first I was scared but now I think it's fine because eating alone today would have me thinking about too many things.

After the other kids leave the room I walk up to Miss Cawl's desk and pull the sandwich out of my backpack. I say, Miss Cawl you said you wanted to see me. She gets up from the desk and closes the door. Her perfume smells like those hy-a-cinth-s at Grandma and Grandpa's. She tells me to sit down and says, Lucas I'm worried about you. She says that my work has been alarming lately. Then Miss Cawl says that not many kids write about death. I say, Dad works with death every day. She says that she knows that and then she asks if I miss Mom a lot and I say I do, a whole lot. Then she asks if anybody else knows that I miss Mom. I say Grandma and Grandpa do. She asks if Dad does and I tell her, I think so. She says maybe her and Dad should talk. I say, OK, and that I think Dad will like her. She says, OK, and that she'll call him after school today. I say, OK, and that he really likes baseball. She says, OK, and tells me to go eat my lunch with the other kids. I don't want to but I say, OK.

Dad didn't say anything about Miss Cawl last night and he's still sleeping. It's already 8:30 and it's a really sunny

Saturday. I think Dad could want to go to the creek today so I try to wake him up. His room smells really bad again and the small silver bottle is on the floor. I pick it up and it's almost empty. When I try to wake him up he coughs and turns onto his side. I nudge him one more time and he says, Not now.

I wait for over two hours and Dad still isn't awake. I go into his room again. His shirt is off now and his small silver bottle is on the floor and when I pick it up this time it's totally empty, which means he'll be asleep for a while longer. But I really want to go outside. I push on his back again and he says, Not now Lukewarm.

I look out the kitchen window at our yard. The grass is really long and probably needs to be cut but Dad doesn't want me cutting the yard by myself so I go into the kitchen and pour a glass of milk and drink that. I wonder if Carlton likes milk as much as I do. I wonder if Carlton likes ice cream. Maybe Carlton likes caramel in his ice cream. Maybe Carlton and his twin went to LaBelle's like Mom and me used to. Maybe Carlton would want to skip stones with me and then go to LaBelle's. He might like it because he might still be sad and he might want to talk about his dead brother and I might want to talk about my dead mom while we eat our ice cream. I could tell him about her hands and we could figure out God's plan for both of us.

I start walking toward where Dad said the dark people live. It's really quiet outside and there aren't too many cars on the road except for next to Roger's Diner, which is really busy on Saturdays. So I look both ways before I cross the road and keep walking toward Grandma and Grandpa's. I remember to walk a street behind their house because I don't want them to see me. If they see me they'll tell me to come inside or they'll call Dad to come and get me because they'll say they are worried about me, just like Miss Cawl. Sometimes it's nice having people worried about you and other times it isn't so nice.

I walk on the sidewalk behind Fred's and it smells so good here and so warm and so much like two Easters ago when Mom and Grandma cooked ham and potatoes and lamb. But through an open door I see some dark men cutting meat on the counter with big knives. I think of Carlton's twin and being stabbed and I start to walk faster. I pass dark women sitting on a picnic table taking pits out of peaches and plums. They smile at me and I smile back. Then I walk past some dark boys playing with a basketball and they are laughing and I start running to them because one of them has orange hair. When I get closer I see it isn't Carlton.

I ask them if they know where Carlton's at and they run away from me, across the street, which makes me sad. It's sad that we run away from people who just want to talk.

Farther up the sidewalk there are some dark people standing outside of the movies. They're all dressed real nice and talking about something they're going to see. Any of the kids move away from me when I walk by so when I see an old man with really thick and smart grey eyebrows I ask him if he knows Carlton. His voice is really scratchy when he says he doesn't know a Carlton and I point to my hair and say, He has orange hair like this. He says, Don't know him, and I say, OK, and walk to another older man and ask him too. He says he doesn't know a Carlton.

When I walk to another old man a woman walks up to me and touches my shoulder and asks me my name. I tell her, I'm Lucas Carlson. She says her name is Loretta. I think that's a good name for her because it makes me think of a tall lady in a pink dress, which is what she is. Loretta asks me what I'm doing today and I say, I'm looking for my friend Carlton. I ask her if she knows him. She says she doesn't know a Carlton. Then she asks why I'm looking for him and I say, Because we're going to skip stones at the creek like Mom and I did 154 days ago. Loretta asks me where Mom is and I tell her Mom has been dead for 121 days. She says she's sorry to hear that. I tell her, It's OK, because Carlton's brother has been dead for three days. She tells me the next time I see Carlton to tell him that she's sorry and I say, I will. I say, Thank you Loretta, and start walking but she stops me and asks where Dad is. I tell her he's still sleeping because he drank over 40 sips from his small silver bottle. Loretta's eyes turn sad. She looks back at the group of people she was standing next to. Then she looks at me and says, Like a flask? I say, What's a flask? She shapes her hands into a square and says, They're silver and people put things that taste like fire into them. I say, That has to be it then. She shakes her head and asks where I live. I tell her, I live 14 blocks away but Grandma and Grandpa live 9 blocks away. She squats down and tells me she wants to see where Grandma and Grandpa live. I grab her hand and tell her I'll show her.

We walk past Jackson's Pharmacy and past Fred's and Loretta asks me how old I am. I tell her, I'll be eight in August. She says, August is a good month, and I say, It sure is. Then a few cars drive by and honk their horns but they don't wave like when me and Dad were playing catch. They just scream words I'm not supposed to say. Loretta looks sad for a minute but asks me what Dad does. I tell her he works at Mr. Xavier's and that he puts big words into dead people and at first all she says is, Oh. Then she asks me what I like to do and I tell her I like to skip stones and that I like wakes and she says that seems odd. I say, I like them because I want to hear more about God's plan. She says she likes that. I tell her, That's where I met Carlton. She says that it sounds like a good place to meet a friend because we all need friends at a time like that. I say, I know.

Both Grandma and Grandpa are outside on their porch and when they see me and Loretta they walk down their steps real fast and grab my hand. Grandma looks like she has been crying. Why would she be crying? Did Grandpa say something mean? Grandpa's voice is never mean. I hug Grandma and say, I don't like it when you cry. Then Loretta says, I'm Loretta, and, It's nice to meet you, and then smiles. Grandma lets go of me and smiles but she doesn't look like she means it. Grandpa asks me where I was. I say, I was looking for Carlton because I wanted to skip stones at the creek like Mom and me used to. Then Loretta says she found me by myself at the movies and that I said they lived here and so she brought me here. Grandpa says, Thank you. Loretta says, You're welcome, and I like how soft her voice sounds when she says it. I say, Thank you Loretta. She says, No problem sweetheart, and I like that she says sweetheart too. Then Loretta walks down the sidewalk alone. All I can think about is how I really want to know what Loretta thinks about when she's alone.

Grandma says, Come inside Lukie, but before we get to the door Dad pulls into the driveway. The car screeches real loud before Dad gets out. Grandpa says, He's OK Walter he's OK, but Dad says, I need to talk to him, and, We're going home. Grandpa starts saying something but Dad says, Not now Mitch, and Grandpa takes Grandma inside. Dad says, Get in the damn car now Lucas, and I do. He gets in and slams his door and starts the car and we take off and he doesn't look at me. He says, What the hell were you doing? What were you thinking? I say, I was looking for Carlton so we could go skip stones at the creek like Mom and me used to. He says, Who the hell is Carlton? I say, Carlton is my friend. I leave out the color of Carlton's skin because I don't want Dad to be any angrier, and I don't want to lie and say that he is white. Dad breathes really heavy and he says, You scared me to death Luke. I say, I didn't want to scare you to death. I really didn't. I don't want Dad to die too. He says, It's OK.

At a stop sign Dad asks me if I miss skipping stones with Mom and I say, Yes. He says, I miss her too. I say, You don't show it. He says, What do you mean? I say, You're too busy, and he doesn't say anything. Then he says, Miss Cawl called the other day to say that she's worried about you. I ask Dad if he likes her and he says, She seems like a nice person. Then Dad asks me what I miss most about Mom. I say, Everything. Then I ask him what he misses most about her. He doesn't say anything for a few seconds but then Dad presses the gas pedal and we start moving again. Then he says, I miss her cheeks. I say, Her cheeks? He says, They were the softest things these hands have ever felt, and he laughs and I laugh and he laughs at me laughing. Then he reaches for his flask and I stop laughing.

RASP

AT APPROXIMATELY 9:00p.m. on February 17th, 2012, seven-month old Cameron Harris was drowned by his mother in a mobile home kitchen sink. Once expired, the mother, Fern (Travettie) Harris, handed her son to her husband, Brian, who proceeded to leave Tamarac Village in his rusted blue 1994 Chevrolet S10. Brian disposed of the body by placing Cameron on a sheet of ice stretching from ditch wall to ditch wall just off of Pere Marquette Road. The police report, as written by the first responder, Mason County Sherriff's Department Deputy Alan Kramer, stated that a sky-blue blanket had been wrapped around Cameron's body, covering all but his head.

Baby Cameron, as he'd become known in the media, was found just after 1:00a.m. on February 18th, 2012 by Zack Strauss. Strauss, a seventeen-year old senior at Ludington High School, said in an interview with the West

Central Gazette minutes after fishtailing off Pere Marquette Road and into the ditch where Baby Cameron lay: "I'd just dropped off my girlfriend, I hit a patch of ice, and-and-and I could've crushed him. Could've just smashed him." Emily Unting, our feature writer at the time, wrote that Zack then clapped once, lightly. "Just like that."

Brian's younger brother, James, scrawny and gap-toothed, stammered in disbelief during his interview with Channel 6, a bit spliced between shots of MCSD officers taking a compliant Brian and Fern into custody: "My brother's the only father I've ever had. He isn't capable of this. No way." He was the only one to cry on camera.

"They deserve to be tied up, those deranged toes inches from the flame," The Silver Fox, a 103.1FM (Petoskey, Michigan) radio personality known for the uncensored music he slipped in during early morning hours stated days after. "Maybe then they'd know the pain they have caused us all." The apology he was forced to make the following night wasn't issued with nearly as much conviction.

Fern's cousin, Lois (Travettie) Henslow, a receptionist for the Hindman/Crown marketing agency in Kalamazoo, placed frustrated hands on narrow hips and said little to Channel 3's cameras before getting into a dented Chevrolet

Trailblazer parked blocks from the office: "She said she needed to talk. I should've listened. But, I ignored her. And now we're here."

Roger Burton, then mayor-elect of Ludington and father of a daughter killed by a drunk driver two years prior, with several microphones inches from his mouth, said to me, to all of us at the news conference outside of Mason County's Courthouse: "Brian and Fern Harris encompass all that is wrong with this world and have brought their evil upon our lovely and safe community. We eagerly await the results of their trial."

For four months the people not just of Ludington, but those across Michigan shouted to one another about Baby Cameron. And what the echos made clear was that they wanted—what the voices truly wanted—was closure through condemnation. They needed someone to blame, and in turn had reacted as if Baby Cameron—a Ludington trailer baby the majority, had it not been for his death, would never know of, or care for—had been deemed the state's child. A part of each citizen had seemingly died along with him.

I didn't share those feelings. I refused to believe that any part of me had died, that a part of me could. Which left me to struggle as I wrote column after column on Baby Cameron, as I worked to wrap my head around the public's reaction. It's interesting now, flipping back through those columns and being able to spot the shifts—in tone, in language, in details—how the first six or so were as cookie cutter as they come, something anyone on staff could've written. I was part of the herd, until questions surfaced that I felt only I could ask and answer. Was all that anger and sadness the public experiencing actually what true empathy was like? And was I incapable? Or was it something contrived, something conjured, something infectious and potent? If it were actually empathy, with whom did they empathize? Us members of the media, for having to cover such a story? The relatives, who hadn't spoken to Brian or Fern for years, let alone burp, change or hold Baby Cameron? Brian and Fern, for having what many speculated must have been a collective chemical imbalance? A seven-month old whose path to royalty had come to an abrupt halt?

On the morning of June 23rd, when Tyler and Celandine Zalinski moved into the cottage across the street from Annie and me, my questions ceased, at least for a day. As I would for the weeks that followed, I watched the Zalinskis through my office window. Their Subaru Outback donned an Indiana license plate, and was the same pale shade of green as their new lawn. Some maple leaves lost in the breeze landed on the roof of the small U-Haul trailer attached to the hitch.

"Honey, I think someone's moving in across the street." The kitchen was only a room over from my office but Annie, as I thought she had for the twenty-one years we'd been married, felt it necessary to shout. "Honey?"

"I see that."

"You know who it is?"

I'd had an idea. Paul Tress, then Sports editor, had said something about Abe Wermer, then editor-in-chief, hiring some new guy from down south. "Finally got someone that knows a thing or two about basketball," Paul had said, though he often questioned Abe's judge of character. Paul estimated that the writers Abe hired for Sports lasted a month before Paul told them to get the hell out, on account that none of them were prepared for the heavy workload a small town sports writer had after the staff had been cut in half.

"You know who it is, Bruce?" Annie repeated. She tiptoed under the office's doorframe, the grey roots I loved clashing with a chestnut dye job she'd done herself six weeks earlier.

"I have an idea, yes."

"Who is it, then?"

I remember refusing to turn and address her. "I'm not sure of the details, Annie," I said, in a tone that hurt her enough that she scurried out of the office.

I watched Ray Sussoman, a sixty-something widower across the street, walk from window to window, rubbernecking for a glimpse of the new neighbors. I imagined the Thurstons, next door to us, doing the same. That's what they did when we moved in. I'd set boxes in the bedroom overlooking our property line and spot Don or Helen in the nearest window, still but featureless. They came over later with chocolate chip cookies and what I'm positive now were feigned smiles reserved for intruders.

For a moment, I wanted to return to my desk, to walk away from the window, if only to cement the differences between us. Yet, and it still isn't easy for me to say this, my time on Piney Ridge Road had shaped me into something I'd never wanted to be. I stayed put, and I stared.

Celandine Zalinski stepped out from the passenger's seat. She'd had on an orange floral dress that stretched tight along her back and hips. Her complexion was sallow. She was short, petite if not for the pregnancy. Which, when Tyler Zalinski stepped out from the driver's seat, made me wonder how she could handle such a man, not just in the bedroom, but if they ever got in an argument that escalated into the pettiest of shoving matches. His neck was thick. The sleeves of his polo shirt could've torn at the bicep. Without turning to address us onlookers, they walked to their new front door and within seconds were inside, empty-handed.

If I were right about the Thurstons, if they were indeed at a window, I don't know what they did after the big reveal. I watched Sussoman shake his head, and then walk back to his game show re-run. I smiled. I smiled because there was a U-Haul instead of some watercraft named "Whistler" or "Skidder" or "Thunderous Wake" or some other machismo name thought up by one of the hundreds of suits from Chicago or Detroit vacationing in Ludington for the summer. I smiled because the Zalinskis weren't a middle-aged couple with spoiled children who complained of the vanishing of service bars on their iPhones as they stepped onto their seasonal driveway. I smiled because they drove that Outback instead of a Range Rover.

Annie opened the office door again around 2:30p.m., holding a cookie sheet. She being so skinny then, the lavender v-neck she'd slipped into hung loose. Exercise was something she'd begun to take seriously a year earlier, including investments into weekly yoga sessions and spin classes at the community college, as well as a workout program ordered from a late night infomercial, all promising Annie the body she already had but refused to truly see.

"When do you wanna go over?"

I took a cookie. "Really? We're like the Thurstons now?"

I had no respect for the Thurstons. That much had been made clear over the years, to both Annie and the Thurstons. The few times Annie and I truly argued—nothing physical, just raised voices and words said and meant but taken back—either Don or Helen, each seeming to be graced with supernatural ears, would stop by after the dust settled and ask about our wellbeing. Which never sat well with me. Our business should be our business, and ours alone, as far as I was concerned, even on the rare occasion that things boiled over.

"It's just a nice thing to do," Annie said. "Are you almost finished with—whatever it is you're working on?"

"Not even close," I said.

Annie set the cookie sheet on the desk. "Come on," she said, stretching her fingers in a way I'd never seen, commanding Word to close my outline of Baby Cameron.

Which stood me up. I smile about the scene now but I know I said, "I didn't even fucking save that" then, and harshly. I'm not proud of it.

Annie was halfway across the street when I caught up. It was muggy outside, with mosquitoes swarming from tree to tree, from swatting hand to swatting hand. Gusts of wind blew beach sand into the road. I scanned the Zalinskis' Outback as we walked by, the Indiana Pacers decal on the back window, the ARMS ARE FOR HUGGING bumper sticker. A stack of Sports Illustrated sat on the back seat. Behind the stack rested a collapsible shovel, and beside it rested woven baskets brimming with wooden kitchen utensils.

Deputy Kramer's report had stated that there was a shovel in Brian Harris's truck. Unused, but present.

Annie, timid with their screen door, knocked on the cottage's siding. A moment later, Celandine appeared. She squinted at my tan Sperrys, her black brows creased with judgment. I stared back, at her bare feet, at the three hemp bracelets dangling from her right ankle. Her stomach was big. Water to break any day now big.

"Hello," Annie said too emphatically. "I'm Annie and this is Bruce. We live across the street."

I gave a smile that matched Annie's, a "nice to meet you" smile I could put on from time to time, for Gazette staff, for neighbors new and old.

Celandine wasn't amused. She stood still, looking like she was on the verge of saying something. In the silence, she rubbed her belly. To calm herself, I'd imagined. It took me back to when Annie was pregnant with Mark, to how she used to rub her belly in grocery store lines and while on the phone. Whenever she felt anxious, wherever she felt stressed. I thought it was such a cute tic, even more so when, years after Mark was born, I'd see Annie instinctively rub the belly that was no longer there, searching for the stress ball she'd lost.

Behind Celandine I saw Tyler walk to the door. He was groggy and rubbing his eyes, his light brown hair messy from a nap. He looked at Celandine with confusion. "Let them in, honey." He smiled at us. "We're the Zalinskis."

Celandine opened the screen door just wide enough for us to squeeze through.

"We made you guys some cookies, a welcome to the neighborhood thing we like to do," Annie said, looking at me like I had helped.

"That's really nice of you," Tyler said. He shook my hand. I still think of them as miller's hands—gritty and callused, plenty of strength to put a man of my size to his knees if he wanted. "Tyler. This is Celandine."

Celandine stepped forward. "Are they organic?"

Annie looked at me like I was supposed to know. "I don't think so," she said.

"We can't eat them," Celandine said.

Tyler looked at each of us apologetically and took the cookie sheet from Annie. "I'll eat them," he whispered, then grabbed a cookie and took a bite.

"Celandine. That's a unique name," I said.

Celandine stared at me. Squint unwrinkled now, her blue eyes looked too cold for a Michigan summer.

"It's very pretty," Annie said.

"She's named after a wildflower," Tyler said. He looked at Celandine's sharp nose, her ears and lips. A look that accepted those eyes for whatever they stood for.

Celandine kept her hand on her belly. "They're in bloom now."

"Like she is," Tyler said, then gave a goofy but proud smile expecting dads think they need to give. Ear-to-ear. "Only a matter of days."

"Do you have any children?" Celandine asked.

"A son. Mark," Annie said. "He just turned nineteen in March."

"College?" Tyler asked.

"Michigan State," I said. "Loving every second, it sounds like."

"He just left on a road trip to Colorado, with his roommates," Annie said.

Which was news to me. "He did?"

Annie nodded. "They left two days ago."

"Fun," Tyler said. "MSU, MSU—played them a couple times when I was at Butler, before we were any good," Tyler said. "Before Coach Stevenson showed up and turned everything around. Could never figure out how to stop their fast break."

I'd heard of Butler, of this Coach Stevenson, so I nodded, but I didn't have anything to add, facts, details, or an opinion. I'd always been interested in athletics, college and professional, but not enough to track stats or remember names of role players.

Unannounced, Celandine grabbed the cookie sheet out of Tyler's hands and walked out of the room, into the kitchen. It was as if she'd been thinking about what she wanted to do for some time, maybe minutes, but chose to stand in silence until something drove her to move. Water apparently, as I listened to her turn the faucet on, the cottage's old pipes revived.

"I could tell you're an athlete," I said. What an awkward thing to say. What an awkward way to break an awkward silence.

"Does Celandine play any sports?" Annie asked. Because Helen Thurston had had hip surgery weeks before on account of "pushing herself too hard" in Pilates, Annie had been looking for a new exercise buddy, but to no avail, the ladies of Piney Ridge Road claiming they had too much on their plate to commit to something like that.

Tyler shook his head. "God, no. She hates sports." He put his hands in his pockets, leaned toward us and quietly said, "I apologize if she was impolite. She's just—she's just always lived way out in the country, away from everything. A lot of new things at once can be overwhelming is all."

"Especially when you're that far along," Annie said.

"Exactly," Tyler said. "That's exactly right."

"She's fine," I said, though I did find it odd for Tyler to apologize for someone he no more than seconds earlier stared at with admiration.

"I'm sure she'll like it here," Annie said. "Lots of rural areas, lots of trees and meadows. The beach is real close, too, obviously. Plenty of outdoorsy things to do."

Tyler smiled. "I think you're right, Annie." He led us into the living room. "Please, relax and take a seat— wherever you can find one."

As we followed Tyler, a mixture of smells whirled about. The open windows let in a musty smell that mingled with the aroma of the cookies. A scent of unwashed running shoes clung to the walls of the old cottage, which was somewhat expected, as we'd watched it wither over time, unoccupied nine months of each year. I leaned against an end table flanking the green rocking chair in which Annie sat.

"So what do you guys do for work?"

"I'm home most days," Annie said, "keeping up with the house and whatnot."

"That's great. That's really great. And you, Bruce?"

"Right now I'm getting into woodcarving. Not good enough to sell them yet, but hopefully it'll pan out," I said, then wondered how unstable it made me sound to announce that first—woodcarver for eight months, columnist for nineteen years. I guess I'd decided to put my eggs in the newest basket; an issue of age, I suppose. Retirement was nearing. News was changing. Its frequency, its medium, so drastically that I'd begun to question how long a columnist with little desire to conform would be able to survive. "That's the next thing, though," I said. "I work at the West Central Gazette. I'm a columnist."

"No shit?" Tyler said. "I start there on Monday. Sports writer."

Having my assumptions confirmed put me at ease. "See, I wondered about that. I saw your license plate and I remembered we hired someone new." I thought again of the Sports Illustrated stack in the Outback. "If you don't mind me asking, why here?"

Tyler thought for a second while he chewed. "I love sports, and I love Michigan. I spent a lot of time here as a kid. Not here, specifically, just all over the state. Applied to the Free Press first and didn't get it. Cel was happy about that. She would've hated Detroit. Ludington wasn't even the second choice, just kind of happened."

Celandine walked into the room with two steaming coffee cups, her head down, focused on not sloshing or spilling. She handed the cups to Annie and me. "Herbal tea," was all she said before she sat next to Tyler on the entertainment center.

"Honey, Bruce here works at the Gazette, too."

"That's nice." Celandine folded her arms as if to say, I guess it's OK for my husband to work there, but you, I despise you for doing so. Celandine, I thought, probably didn't read or watch the news, had no respect for those working to keep the people in the know, had no idea what was going on nearby unless a sawn maple split her home when it fell.

"At least you two can carpool now," Annie said, trying to find a spot in the conversation to jump in. "Bruce just goes in on Mondays and works at home the rest of the week."

I told Annie later that she shouldn't have said that. Going to the office one day a week made me sound lazy. There were several writers doing the very same thing, though, replaced by citizen journalists who pitched stories like the First Methodist Church Bake Off or the ever-changing management of a thrift store—and get them, as well as likes and comments and shares and whatever the hell else notoriety required at the time.

"Carpooling is the least you can do if it isn't within walking or biking distance," Celandine said to Tyler. It was nice to hear some emotion instead of imagining where she hid it.

Tyler nodded agreement, then turned to me. "What do you know about that Baby Cameron story? Whole car ride that's all we heard."

No one outside of the newspaper had asked me directly about Baby Cameron, not even Annie. Nothing about the facts, nothing about the details. Nothing of my then-unformed opinion. "I'm writing a column about it right now," Despite her never asking me about my columns, despite her force-quitting my document before we ventured here, I found calmness by looking at Annie. "I've written nearly a dozen now, actually."

"No shit?" Tyler said. He liked that phrase.

"Yeah," I said. "Messy stuff."

"As fun as messy can be," Celandine said, her voice louder now. "Let's not talk about that here." She looked at Tyler, then at her belly, and then at Annie. "How's your tea?"

I picked Tyler up to go to the office the following Monday. Celandine was near their lone elm tree and in that same dress from Saturday, pushing clothes in a bucket of soapy water with a stick, then hanging them on a line she strung from the elm to a nearby oak after rinsing them out in a different bucket. I didn't think much of it, honestly, given that I hadn't seen a washer or dryer in the cottage the day Annie and I brought them cookies, nor had I seen a delivery truck of any sort in the days that followed. What I did find odd was the way that Celandine ignored me. She didn't look my way until Tyler came out of the cottage. He waved at me from the doorstep before he walked over and gave

Celandine an "I'm off to work" kiss. Tyler then said something to her, maybe an "I'll miss you" or "Don't miss me too much", something generic I didn't think Celandine would smile at. But she did and it didn't come on suddenly and it left in no hurry.

"Morning," Tyler said, passenger door ajar. Once he sat down, he yawned and rubbed sleep from his eyes.

"Not much of a morning person?"

"Never sleep well on the couch." He waved at Celandine as we backed out.

"Sleep there often?"

Tyler yawned again. "Throughout the pregnancy, yeah. Cel isn't a great sleeper to begin with. Add in that level of discomfort and, well, you get it."

I nodded. I did get it.

"I mean, there's more to it," Tyler said. "There's more." He was quiet for a few seconds, debating the next words out of his mouth. "You saw it, you heard it: Celandine cares about the world. She cares about her health, my health, the baby's health. She cares deeply about balance." Tyler laughed. "It's infuriating sometimes, but I love that about her. I love that it so isn't how I think."

So that's how they'd come to be, I thought. Celandine gave Tyler a break from stadiums, obnoxious fans and jock straps. She'd insisted on talking about herbs or dandelions instead of final scores and draft prospects. She'd challenged him.

"Sometimes, though, I wonder if that's going to be a good thing when the baby comes, those differences. Take me, for example," Tyler said. He seemed to wake up then. "I love sports. I love cars. I love being near a city."

I wasn't sure why Tyler had decided to have this conversation with someone he'd met only days before. But, without him communicating it, I somehow understood I was the only person he could have it with, that he was desperate for someone in which to confide. Based on my lone interaction with her, I assumed Celandine would shut down as a listener, would snatch the conversation and take it elsewhere.

"But Cel, she hates sports, hates cars, hates the city." Tyler looked out the window for a while. "She even thought this place was too big. Too polluted. Too populated. And of course it isn't but—." He trailed off. "They say opposites attract, which is as true as can be with Cel and me. But to a kid, opposites are confusing, right? You know what I mean, Bruce?"

I knew. When we first started dating, what Annie had (money from Daddy, who'd been co-owner of an auto company until the recession took it under) and believed in (romance, which was what her parents were able to demonstrate over three family vacations per year, one to Miami, one to Chicago, one to Traverse City), was damn near the opposite of what I had (minimal finances, at best, thanks to a two-packs-a-day-at-the-kitchen-table mom and a nail gun dad) and believed in (work ethic, which had helped bring me out of Saginaw poverty). She had never been anything like Celandine—she would never refuse freshly baked cookies from neighbors, wash clothes by hand or make me sleep on the couch.

Degrees of our differences were presented to Mark early on. For a while he seemed to side with Annie, who talked to the walls about recent PTA meetings while she did his homework for him, who took him to the beach as a youngster and encouraged him to play soccer with boys his age, driftwood as goalposts. But as he grew older, he seemed to shift. I'd take him to the same beach some mornings, and we'd hardly talk, but just watch what was going on—the sun-risers packing up their gear, the spot-claimers setting theirs down, the joggers, those waving their metal detectors down by the shore. I wouldn't help with homework, didn't participate in any organizations—I'd been passive, wanting, expecting Mark to observe, to refine the tools it took to teach one's self, to formulate his own opinions about the world and the people within it.

Were we opposites? Did we present the idea of opposites to Mark? I don't think so. I think we what we gave Mark was the gift of multiple perspectives. It's possible that it could've been confusing to him, then. But I'd argue that a child with a wide variety of experiences will benefit later. I do still wonder sometimes, though, whether it was Annie or I who played a more crucial role in shaping Mark.

"What you're thinking about is normal," I said. "The fears that come with being a parent won't go away. You just have to take it all as it is." I turned onto Lakeshore Drive, the road Brian and Fern once lived on, the road that would take us all the way to the office, past Lakeview Cemetery and its headstone meadows. "You and Celandine are going to be just fine."

On Wednesday morning, I needed a rest from Baby Cameron. Though I've given it up now, woodcarving was my escape at the time. Something requiring complete concentration, something that shielded the outside noise. I'd try to carve fish, and dreamt often about the day I'd finish a salmon, or pike, or halibut. I'd become quite excited when I allowed myself to imagine a piece mine in an office, or in a living room, mounted with pride by someone who'd seen the value in my craft. It took me two years to realize my hands weren't fit for such things.

I waited for Don Thurston's Lexus to leave his driveway, then opened the garage door to let in the breeze. While I trimmed a couple blocks of cedar with the bandsaw, I noticed Celandine in her yard. She just stood there, a dozen feet from the road, arms down, nose pointed at the sky. I wondered what she was thinking, what she was saying, if anything, if her lips were moving at all. Part of me hoped she was summoning some sort of rain-inducing abilities meant to break the streak of humidity, that soon enough she'd skip across the grass with one arm in the air, chanting incoherencies.

She turned her attention to me once I killed the bandsaw. She didn't smile and neither did I, but I felt obligated to at least wave. Without returning the wave—again that suddenness, as if she had been thinking about how best to approach—she walked over, head down, not even bothering to look one way or the other while crossing the road.

"Hi there," I said.

Celandine said hello, but then walked in the garage and silently looked at the ceiling, at the lone window, at the pile of wood I had next to me.

I grabbed a rasp off the bench. "Ever tried it?"

She shook her head. "Why?"

"Why? Why try it?"

She rubbed her belly and talked through a long exhale. "Why do you do it?"

"Guess I just like to." She looked away again. The Outback wasn't in the driveway. "How's Tyler?"

"He's fine."

I wondered what "Fine" meant to Celandine. Was she fine? In her mind, was she at this moment its definition? "Are you okay, Celandine? Is Tyler around today?" I asked.

She touched her belly. "He's at a baseball game in Mu-ske-g—."

"Muskegon?"

She nodded. "Yes." She even laughed at her pronunciation. And, as brief as it was, I saw how attractive she could be, guiding her hair behind her ears, revealing a smile I couldn't help but find incredibly rewarding, something you had to work for but something so rare, something authentic you strove to witness it with regularity.

It communicated to me without her having to say so that, yes, Celandine was okay.

I relaxed. I started moving the rasp over the rough edges of the wood. "The job will take him all over the place. Just part of the deal."

Celandine struggled over her belly to grab a block of wood from the pile. Crouched, she said: "You should plant a tree for each one you carve."

"Oh yeah?"

"More and more forests are being depleted every day. You know that, right?"

There it was, her spiel. I expected a lecture that was supposed to make me feel horrible for having a hobby that involved a natural resource. "All I make is fish." I showed her how small the carvings actually were, a bit longer than my hand.

"Why fish?" Oddly, the question didn't ring of accusation, or instruction, but rather some hardened form of curiosity.

"They say it's the easiest thing to make for beginners"

She struggled to stand but waved off my assistance. "Is that true, that it's easy for beginners?"

I smiled. "Not really."

She returned the smile. "Can I see that piece, in your lap?"

It was basically a rectangle, save for one side being rounded down. I handed it to her. "It's not even close to being finished."

"Do you know when it'll be perfect?"

"Perfect? I don't think it'll ever be perfect." I watched her rotate the wood. She handed it back to me, then walked out of the garage without another word.

###

Because the first jury had been exposed by some citizen journalist (a Walgreens cashier by day) up from Coldwater who posted a courtroom photo to Yahoo!, a new jury for the Baby Cameron trial was being selected that Thursday. I didn't go to the selection because it wouldn't have helped me anyway—new faces wouldn't help make Baby Cameron clear.

The mistake, however, confirmed what I wanted to accomplish with this Baby Cameron column: readers needed to be challenged. A different perspective needed to be presented, where there were no sides and few questions were answered. I needed to grapple with the reader, force them to alter their posture, to reposition the weak stance they maintained. I needed to show them Brian and Fern's actions were not right, but that what is right and what is wrong is a complex construction of our minds, honed over years, over tragedy, over joy.

Lofty aim, to be sure, with a high degree of risk involved. Modern readers, as I'd been told by editorial time and again, weren't looking to be challenged. If the goal is clicks, sure, write a challenging headline. But to challenge them over the course of paragraphs? Over the course of pages? No, what modern readers were looking, according to the newspaper's editor-in-chief, Abe Wermer, was validation.

"Ask yourself then, Bruce," Abe had said the first and second times I pitched the idea of challenging our readers, "how much are you willing to pay to be told you're wrong? Tell me, how much. What's the price tag there? Because, as much as I wish it weren't the case, the roof over our heads is top of mind for me. And our roof, as you know, is on fire. The only thing that can put that fire out is subscriptions. Not Pulitzers."

He'd gone on to lecture me about community building, about the type of reader the Gazette wanted for the long haul, broken down by demographics, heaps of data split by our analytics team in dozens of ways. And I was listening. I heard him. I thought his viewpoint valid. Valid, but infuriating. Survival of the Gazette was Abe's primary goal, no matter what shape that meant the Gazette had to take. But, for me and what I brought to the table, the game Abe wanted to play was dangerous. What role can a columnist play when the directive is that all opinions must be the same? What value—true value—can a columnist add in a homogenous environment? At the expense of my dignity, not to mention the job I'd held for nearly two decades, what Abe was asking me to do, whether he realized it or not, was to tighten the leash around my neck and slowly lead myself to the slaughterhouse.

Which I wasn't yet ready to do.

So, I watched and re-watched interviews with those closest to Brian and Fern: James Harris, Lois Henslow and a childhood friend, Brock Steffes, who contacted Channel 6 after hearing of the murder, insisting he had information vital to the case. All he shared were memories of he and Brian playing tag on an elementary playground when they were nine years old. Brian was fast back then. Brock was slow. End of story.

With neither of Brian's parents living and Fern's too distraught to comment, these were the three sources from which I chose to pull. These were the three because the fact of the matter was that Brian and Fern had chosen to be outsiders. Not even their neighbors knew much about them. They claimed Brian and Fern to be good neighbors, quiet neighbors, the introverted, stay-at-home-and-binge-on-Netflix type.

To pay for their lot at Tamarac, Brian filled in at Vern Boorman's cherry farm in Scottville when work was available. But that was all. No second job. According to Lois, Fern refused to work.

A Hispanic coworker of Brian's, Thiago Morales, told me, "[Brian] always had his headphones in," when I asked about the conversations they shared. "You can ask any of us. He didn't talk much," he said. "He'd just smoke, listen to music and trim trees."

Search teams had found small quantities of marijuana taped to the inside of the mobile home's kitchen and bathroom counters, tucked in the glove compartment of Brian's S10. In their living area were stacks of vintage records but no record player. The likes of Los Bravos, Ian Whitcomb, The Kingsmen, obscure 60s artists that to my knowledge had never been touted as the next best thing, let alone by Brian and Fern's generation.

That night, as I squeezed a tension ball, I convinced myself that this column would be my take, that it should be my take. No one else's. Everyone else had had their say and, as instructed, I'd echoed it as far and wide as I could. But not this time.

I convinced myself that there were no more meaningful facts of the Baby Cameron case to include, that they'd all been used up, that things like Baby Cameron's murder happen across the country, and often. Happen to couples who love. Happen to couples who love, then hate, then love each other again in a matter of hours. But infanticide doesn't just occur because of fluctuating emotions. It can't. There has to be influence from something else. Someone else—relatives, parents, grandparents, friends, whomever hints at the incapability of successfully raising a child, an insecurity planted deep in the brain. But to introverted outsiders like Brian and Fern, what does successfully raising a child mean? More importantly, who or what told them they weren't capable?

And what of the death? Something could surely be said about how Fern killed her son. Could I say it was better that she drowned Baby Cameron instead of having Brian grab his arms and fling him against a car door? Could I say it was better Brian put Baby Cameron in a ditch next to one of the most driven roads in Mason County so he could be found quickly instead of placing him in the woods where coyotes would tear him to shreds?

"Nice and slow," I heard Tyler say outside. My window was partially open.

"I want to have it here."

From the office window I watched Tyler guide Celandine down their front steps.

"Honey, we've been over this. We can't have it here." Tyler opened the passenger door of the Outback for her. "They told us that months ago, remember?"

Celandine stood under the porch light. "I don't want their drugs," she said. I held onto this thought for some time afterward, wondering if one day I'd be able to spot rows of cannabis planted behind the cottage.

"Just get in the car, Cel."

For a moment I think Celandine saw me watching from the window, noticed the two pried blinds. I know she did. I know she saw me and I know that's why she got in the car. Which brought back memories, of Sussoman and the Thurstons watching from their porches as I hustled Annie to the car, a pressure I not once sought heaping on my shoulders by the second.

###

The next afternoon, I watched Tyler jog into his house with an empty canvas bag I assumed he'd pack with organic food Celandine requested from her hospital bed. When Tyler came back out, he looked tired as hell. Shoulders slumped, clothes wrinkled from sleeping in a bedside chair, hair jutting out like a bluejay's.

I said through my open office window: "Slow down, big guy."

Confused, Tyler searched for where the voice came from. I think it could've been this kind of naïveté that drew me to Tyler. Celandine knew exactly where to look.

"It's Bruce," I said. "How is everything?"

Tyler located my window. "It's good. Everyone's healthy. Just grabbing a few things."

"Boy or girl?"

"Girl," he called out. As Tyler got into the car, I spotted a folded sky blue blanket tucked under his arm and it made me think of Deputy Kramer's report, then wonder if Celandine had planned on a boy, had declined to know its sex but had held onto a hunch.

Annie walked into the office with our dog, Jess, a two-year old mutt Mark brought home as a present for Annie before he went off to college, citing that his mom needed something to take care of once he was gone. "Who are you yelling at?" she asked, getting Jess's leash ready for their routine walk around Hamlin Lake.

"Tyler. They had a girl."

After Mark, Annie had always wanted a girl. "That's great," Annie said, and for a moment I think I could see envy reach across her cheeks. "Maybe it'll soften Celandine up a bit."

###

That Saturday was beautiful. Little humidity, not a cloud in the sky and somewhere near seventy-five degrees, Annie, along with most of the neighborhood, was outside. Jess was tied up under the shade of our maples by the road, panting when not barking at dogs and their walkers passing by. The Thurstons sat in patio chairs near their mailbox. Sussoman wrestled with some weeds in his one flower bed of petunias and chrysanthemums. Annie worked on her rosebush below the office window, trimming heavy branches that had made it lean east. I watched her work the sheers, admired the wrinkles on her triceps that she wished would go away. The rest of the neighbors, I assumed, were by the lakeshore, on beach towels, or on the sandbar splashing water at each other. I even heard a powerboat, probably "Whistler," skidding across its own wake and thought it a peaceful thing.

All day I'd been sitting in my office wondering if ever I could put myself in the shoes of Brian and Fern Harris, if I could find it in me to kill my own son, either as the pudgy baby that he was or as the thin blonde-bearded young man he'd become. There was no way. Just contemplating it nauseated me. But that didn't mean that it was completely immoral for Brian and Fern. Did it?

What I was stuck on: I took a philosophy class in college that gave students a hypothetical situation. You were in a burning art museum and you could either choose to save the Mona Lisa from one room, or save an abandoned baby from another. You could only carry one. You had to ask yourself, "What would be better for the world? Most of my classmates sided with saving the baby, their argument being that it's a life that has yet to be lived, full of potential good. But I, as well as a guy named Duncan, chose the Mona Lisa.

Duncan proceeded to argue that the money made by selling the Mona Lisa to the highest bidder, it being the world's most valuable painting, could provide food, water, and shelter to thousands of people in need. "It was the humanitarian thing to do," Duncan had said.

I didn't disagree. But that wasn't my argument. I chose the Mona Lisa because Adolf Hitler had once been an infant. And Timothy McVeigh. And Osama bin Laden. I chose the Mona Lisa because one should not ignore the opposite of the argued potential good. I chose the Mona Lisa because the fact that a baby is stranded doesn't mean that one day they won't perform acts of evil, however catastrophic.

On her evaluation of our arguments' strength, the professor deemed myself and Duncan the victors. When class was dismissed, there was a young woman—I don't recall her name—who came up to me with wet eyes, her finger pointed at my chest. "Baby killer," she said. And she said it one more time before walking off.

I figured I'd add that anecdote somewhere in the column, maybe even start with that girl pointing her finger at me. But the more I thought about the Mona Lisa, the more I kept seeing Mark as a baby. His eyes, I swear, were the size of bottle caps, his hair silky, his feet only a third of my hand. Not once did I think this child of mine could hurt anyone, destroy anything, not with those feet, not with those hands or tongue. He was only capable of building and helping and being kind and decent.

I went back to the death of Baby Cameron, the actual act of murder. Neither parent had appeared to act out of hate. A violent act fueled by hate would've resulted in blood or bruising. Several stabs of a knife. Shoving him through a wood chipper. That wasn't what happened. Not that a seven-month old could put up much of a fight, but there were no bruises. No scrapes, no fingernail marks.

"Must've just held 'em down gently," the medical examiner, Irvine Lang had told me, when I believed facts would serve as the spine of the column. He shaped his large, gloved hands into the position he imagined Fern using. "Minimal pressure on either the head or lower back. They were careful not to use force."

Is there morality in that? And, if the murder was not committed out of hate, what was it then? Fear? And what were the origins of that fear? Maybe they saw some kind of emotional blemish in their son the night he was born, something that planted within them a feeling that the kid would discard every opportunity to come his way, that he'd evolve into the next Manson or Bundy. Maybe they saw him one day reaching for his steak knife at the dining room table and running the blade across his arm. Maybe at six months old he'd banged his head on the floor repeatedly instead of trying to crawl. Could violence inflicted upon the self be a sign? Not that early, right? Still, left to the imagination were scenes of Brian and Fern passing a bowl, eating microwaved dinners and watching their son, sharing a stare that said it was time.

My cell phone rang. It was Mark. I'd called him earlier that day. The thought of murdering him had made me long to hear his voice. He was out of breath when he answered.

"Something wrong, Mark?"

"No, no, I'm fine. Just had to run up a hill to get service." He yelled to one of his roommates to be quiet. "You called earlier. What's up?"

"Been busy. Your mom, too." Mark yelled for someone to grab him a beer, which wasn't something he'd do if Annie were on the line. He was nineteen at the time, almost twenty—I knew underage drinking would happen and had accepted that fact, had even convinced myself that it was better for him to binge at nineteen than at twenty-nine. Get it out of his system. Still: "You guys being careful?"

"Of course, Dad. Listen, can I call you back? About to get back on the road, and I'm losing you."

###

It had been Tyler's turn to drive into the office, but I insisted I give the new father a break. I picked him up and, as gloomy as that Monday was, as gloomy as it could've been for him, with his parental leave nixed, to this day I still haven't seen him so giddy. He told me they'd named her Ivory. He told me again and again how beautiful she was, how indescribable of a feeling it was to hold her, to have his finger wrapped by her hand. I was happy for him. I said so. Told him to cherish such things.

"Zalinski, you get that piece about the Bobcats done?" Paul Tress asked as we walked into the office. Paul—broad shoulders, toucan nose, big gut buoyed by suspenders—was an intimidating man, but even more so when growling questions like this.

"Mr. Tress, I apologize, but no, no I don't have it done," Tyler said. Paul settled his weight on his heels and crossed his arms. "My baby girl was born this weekend."

"I know. I know." Paul sighed. Seemed to bat scenarios around in his mind about how to handle everything. "Just get the story to me by this afternoon, if you can," Paul eventually said. He nodded at me. "Newhouse, good to see ya."

"You believe that guy?" Tyler asked me after Paul was out of earshot.

I chuckled. "He likes you."

Abe Wermer appeared soon after Paul walked away and, right on cue, said: "Bruce, where are you at with the new Baby Cameron column?" Thin and pointy, I'd always likened Abe to a swizzle stick. "We're going on two weeks now." I knew that all too well.

"Making some headway," I said. Over the weekend, I had, but not as much as Abe would've liked. He'd preached time and again that in today's world quantity was far more important than quality.

"Well, we all hope so. Tick tock," Abe said. Then he slithered back to his office and shut the door.

"Can you believe that guy?" I said. Tyler found that very funny.

I sat at a vacant desk near Tyler's. My working primarily from home for the past months had been Abe's suggestion, a way to cut office costs. But in doing so, I discovered through reflection that I'd always found it difficult to get any work done at the office. When I started at the Gazette the problem had been how noisy the place was, the incoherent chatter, the constant punching of keys. But then it had become increasingly difficult because of that noise fading away, the emptiness that came with a slashed staff. All would be quiet except for three or four employees lightly typing on laptops or conducting interviews over office phones.

On his way to the coffee pot, Tyler stopped at the desk I was at. "I think me and Cel will bring her by tomorrow, after I get back," he said. "If that's okay with you."

I told him that Annie and I would love to see her.

He smiled as he walked off. "My family, will be coming over," he said and continued to practice while walking. "My family."

But they never did.

It was approximately 11:15p.m on Tuesday night when the Zalinskis' porch light came on. I walked to the window and watched a shadow, Tyler's—too big of a body to be Celandine—walk along the driver's side of the car. His right arm was chickenwinged, edges of that same sky blue blanket swaying. I could barely make anything else out before he arrived at the car. Only a bit of his face: his eyes, his mouth. From this distance, from this angle, for that split second that he looked down at the blanket, all I could register was that they looked incredibly sad. I watched him open and close the driver's side door, start the car and back out of the driveway.

I called the Zalinskis' cottage. No answer. No interior lights flipped on, not even when I walked over and knocked

on the door. No one rustled around inside. No baby cried.
Tyler had to have her—that's what he was carrying. But
why? Where was he going? Diapers? Formula? The curves of
Pere Marquette Road?

Walking back to the house, I thought of the Baby
Cameron photos kept from the public, one in particular
given to me upon request showing Baby Cameron's bare
head frozen to a piece of ice. Once broken by Strauss's
vehicle, the ice angled towards the bottom of the ditch.
There were splotches of skin where Baby Cameron's head
had ripped away. His eyelashes had turned into tiny icicles.

I didn't want to wake Annie. There was no need, let
alone time, so within minutes I was backing the Corolla out
of the garage.

There were a few other cars on the road, some heading
north, some south and all traveling much slower than me.
When the Outback came into sight, I slowed down. I don't
know why. I could've driven alongside Tyler and pointed to
the shoulder of the road but I didn't, and I don't know why.
I could've made him stop but I didn't, and I don't know
why. Doing so would've saved so much time. Instead of
confronting him then and there, I hung back until the
Outback turned right onto M-116, then followed.

Had Tyler ever been north of Ludington? Or west? Did he even know where he was going? Where was Celandine sending him? Or maybe this was Tyler ditching her plan. Maybe this was Tyler improvising. But Celandine killed that baby. I knew she had. Tyler couldn't have done it. He'd been too happy, too damn happy. I imagined a birthmark on the neck she despised, a shortened finger that couldn't be corrected, an imperfection not even a rasp could smooth.

I noticed breaks in thin clouds. The tops of trees outlining the State Park. The moon, stars here and there. Other than the taillights of the truck, some Ford I kept between myself and Tyler, it was the only light. Once the truck turned right into a large parking lot by public restrooms and picnic tables, I slowed down again. I don't know why I was so adamant on keeping distance between us, but I did, and it allowed me to see the lake between gaps in tree branches. It was calm and it made me question my participation in this, if this was the columnist in me, the father, the friend, or if distinction between one another was even possible.

A couple miles later Tyler turned left into the parking lot of Big Point Sable, a non-working lighthouse turned tourist attraction. I knew, I just knew he was going to leave his daughter here, where she could be found easily by some cubicle dweller on a morning jog, by some kid whose errantly-thrown football dinged the dead girl's forehead. Police cars. News vans. Months of speculation. Repeat.

Tyler drove to the front of the empty parking lot, parked, and shut the car off. The interior light came on in the Outback. His head turned toward the road. I drove a couple hundred yards further, away from Tyler, so as not to be spotted. I parked far away, shut my headlights off, and continued watching Tyler. He opened the Outback door and stepped out, his arm chickenwinged once more. I watched him walk toward the lighthouse, and then shifted back into drive and slowly made my way toward the front of the parking lot, headlights still off.

Now out of my car, I looked through the dark windows of Outback. There was nothing out of the ordinary in the back seat—an empty car seat, the same stack of Sports Illustrated, the same woven baskets now empty, granola bar wrappers, and sunglass cases. There was no baby bottle, no blankets, no box of diapers, no rattles. But there no longer was the collapsible shovel. Because the shovel was in his free hand. It had to be. He wasn't just going to set her on the ground; Tyler was going to bury his daughter.

I don't know what I planned on doing but, because I didn't immediately dial 911, I must've maintained some level of doubt. Not enough for me to stop telling myself that I couldn't let that happen, whatever it was that was happening. I couldn't turn the other way and run. And does that make me fine? Does that make me better than fine? Does that make me decent?

I walked toward the lighthouse. The wind was colder there than at home and I heard waves rolling to shore, breaking sporadically. Dune grass shivered atop mounds of sand on each side of the boardwalk leading to the lighthouse. A freighter's beacon of light shone way off in Lake Michigan, which made me think of shipwrecks, of Tyler and his dead daughter and what happened, what Celandine saw wrong. But then I heard a wail, a grown man's wail. I waited until I heard another one, then tried to locate where it came from. Walking toward the sound, I pictured Celandine filling the kitchen sink and holding the baby by her feet until she stopped wiggling. Plugging the nose, covering her mouth with bare hands. I walked further, wondering if I'd somehow played a part in this.

A gust of wind.

Our conversation in the garage. She'd wanted her baby to be perfect. But it wasn't. It couldn't be.

Waves breaking.

I looked to my left and saw a silhouette sitting atop the sand.

Wind. Waves.

I walked closer. My voice cracked when I said, "Tyler?"

The silhouette shifted. "Bruce?"

I looked at Tyler's lap, where Ivory lay, blades of dune grass inches from her ears. Her face was expressive. Her legs moved.

"Bruce, are you okay?"

"It's just that you, uh, you guys didn't come over today." Tyler adjusted his posture. The baby girl's head moved. Her eyelashes moved. Everything moved. "And when I saw you leave I—I." I put my hands on my hips and looked out at the lake. I felt my stomach turning on itself. "I'm sorry," I said, wiping my mouth.

"I'm sorry I didn't let you know. I totally spaced. Little miss Ivory here has been pretty restless." Tyler ran his fingers through what little hair she had. "Paul didn't seem too happy when I called in but he said he understood. Now that Cel's finally asleep I wanted to give her some peace and quiet, you know?" Tyler caught me staring at Ivory's feet, at the pink socks covering ten wiggling toes.

I flattened some dune grass next to Tyler and sat down. Sand trickled past the tongues of my shoes and it made me calmer, sinking. At that moment I tried to remember where the Mona Lisa was. France, I was sure. The Louvre. But I didn't care, really. Let the painting burn. "So Celandine's doing okay then?"

"She's just exhausted. I mean, she was exhausted before labor. Tack that on, and then adjusting to a new home life, I'm sure it'll take a little time."

A decent person taking their turn in this conversation would have said that Celandine was going to be fine, that she'd be a great mother, maybe that she already was. But I couldn't bring myself to. Each detail disproving what I'd expected, what I'd tricked myself into believing made me feel like a harpooned sturgeon brought on deck to be cut open.

"I'm sorry," I said.

"For what, Bruce?"

I wanted to confess my troubles with Baby Cameron to Tyler. I wanted to tell him how confused I was that Ivory was fine, that I would've been relieved if his baby girl were dead because that would've made me feel certain about at least one thing. "When I was walking up, I thought I heard you crying."

"Crying? Really? No, no, I was humming," Tyler said, straightening his legs slowly, Ivory descending with them. "I guess we were a little loud, weren't we, little girl?"

That was a cry, I knew it was a cry. He couldn't have been humming, a hum couldn't be so loud. "What were you humming?"

"It's cheesy," he said. "You'll laugh. 'Row, Row, Row Your Boat'. She loves that song. Well, I think she does anyway." Tyler offered Ivory to me. "You want to give it a shot?"

I forced a smile. "You go ahead."

Tyler hummed, and it was loud, until that freighter tugged its horn. Ivory cried at the deep sound. Tyler lifted her and swayed her back and forth until her crying subsided.

We talked about the Gazette for a while, about Tyler's next big assignment (Ludington High School football offseason workouts) until Ivory fell asleep, then walked to the parking lot. I'd been so far in my head that I'd left the Corolla running.

"I'll be right behind you," Tyler said, setting Ivory into her car seat carefully.

"Look." I had to say it again. "I'm really sorry. I'm not usually like this." No, the usual Bruce packed himself tightly in his office and stared out a window to assume, to speculate, to tell himself lies about things he thought he understood.

"Bruce," Tyler said. "Stop apologizing. We're friends, right? I'm sure it looked suspicious as hell, me loading up a newborn late at night and driving off." Tyler patted my back and had I not had my feet shoulder width apart, I may have toppled over. "It's great here though, isn't it?"

"Yeah."

Tyler followed until I stopped at a Wesco and bought a cup of coffee. Before I went in the house, I rearranged tools and swept sawdust in the garage because that's all I felt like doing, that's all I felt I was capable of. Annie woke up to me rounding out a fish's sides so I told her, "I couldn't sleep," over and over until she, still concerned, went into the house. I called Mark's cell phone and told his voicemail I loved him, wherever he was, whomever he decided to become. And before I went to bed, I wrote by hand not about Baby Cameron, but about the Zalinskis, about neighbors, about how the Harrises had conditioned me to think of mine as murderers. I wrote that I was wrong and circled it at least twenty times.

HEEL TO LUNG, EAR TO EAR

ODELL ISN'T FUCKING you the way you told him to. Not once have you requested these slow thrusts, nor have you asked for his eyes to hover over yours and stare—stare until his thin orange brows angle with concern, embers misled by the night. You want to tell him is that he doesn't need to do that, that there is no camera, to stop propping himself on one elbow and grazing your nipple with his calloused thumb. You want to tell him not to press his windburnt lips to your collarbone. You want to tell him that this is no time or place for attempts at love.

What you think you want—have wanted since Rex, have wanted for months, well before you unbuttoned Odell's pants, stroked, then guided his small dick inside of you and said, not whispered, "Fuck me like you hate me."—what you think you need is for Odell to look away, at the snow-dusted pines, at the last breaths of the bonfire, at the stars, at the goddamn moons of Jupiter. You need that calloused thumb not on your nipple, but on your windpipe, and you need that thumb to squeeze, to squeeze like hell, to roll the bliss of this out of you as if it were the last gobs of Crest in its tube. Because this, you have learned, whatever this is, whatever this mutates into, no matter how near paradise stretches of this could be, this will end in pain.

Instead, you lie. You tell him how great this feels. You tell him how big he is. You moan. You nod. You writhe on the pickup's bed to get him deeper, to motivate him to go faster. Your right shin bashes Odell's stray belt buckle, its sound tinny, hollow. A cup clanged along prison bars. You shuffle the lies, you shuffle all that roams inside, heel to lung, ear to ear.

And you conjure an image of you and Odell months from now, walking beneath the glitter-and-sequined PROM arch, he in a tux and you in that strapless green dress your mother promised she'd work doubles for. You grin at the way the strobe lights glint off of your grandmother's emerald earrings. You laugh at how he spills spiked punch on his crooked bowtie. You lick a piece of cloth and dab the stain out. You grab his drunk hands and wrap them around your waist so that the two of you can sway like willow branches. Sway and think of—

—you and Odell in a crowded movie theater showing for one night only some horror flick he'd has been dying to see. You hate horror movies but haven't told him that yet. You haven't told him that it doesn't matter how unbelievable the plot is, or how dumb the characters are, when you're anywhere near imagery like that you could go days without sleep. On screen, a bare-breasted twenty-something sprints through a dense forest, screaming for something, for a paved road, for a lover, for civilization, for something nobody cares about. You decide to keep your hands busy. You fan your jacket over Odell's lap and search for his zipper beneath. Odell starts tonguing the tip of her ear once you have his dick out and hard. Stroke it. Stroke, and grin, at how loud he's being, at how far he tilts his head back, at the vascularity of his neck.

This is all you do: grin, stroke.

It's all you'll do when you eat dinner with Odell's family. You'll see the stress of the day, of the week, of the decade, in his mother's eyes, and you'll smell the pig shit on the folds of his father's jeans, but you'll grin because later Odell will lead you to his bedroom, unbutton his plaid shirt, and sit in his office chair, hoping that you'll follow, that you'll fling your thong at the closet door and fuck him there. And you will. You'll straddle him. You'll guide it in. You'll graze his chest with your fingernails and you'll arch your back and you—

—don't listen. Don't. You never do. Ignorant, that's what you are. Of just how cold it really is tonight, in the bed of this truck. Ignorant of the sound the aluminum beer cans eek when punctured by flame, of yet another four-wheel-drive crunching over unpacked snow and parking alongside the corn silo, of the open hand slaps on the pickup's quarter panels, of your classmates' slurred squeals of "Atta boy!" and "Fuck her harder, you bitch!"

Fuck her harder. You bitch.

Listen to that. Slow that down. Speed that up. Fuck-her-harder-you-bitch. Slow it down again. Turn your mind into a scalpel and separate vowel from consonant. Dig for meaning but extract only wonder. Wonder why you liken the dead tree branches above to deer antlers. Wonder what your little brother is doing, whether at this very moment he is jerking off into yet another one of your ankle socks, or if he, like last week, and the week before, is sitting up in bed on a Saturday night, waiting to hear your footsteps before he turns out his light. Think of your remaining grandfather, his khaki fedora that he still tilts so his age-puffed eyes can rest in shade. Wonder if he knows what you do. Wonder if he knows more about who you are than you ever will. Wonder what brought you here. Not the shots of cheap vodka you slammed, not the two beers Odell gave you, not Kaila's chained Escort tires, not even her elegant, "Fucking come on already, Carin. We need us some man."

No. Go deeper. Dart past the quiche you made for Odell in home-ec., past how grateful he was for you getting him a B+, past how he grabbed your hand and tacked, "I owe you one," to his awkward announcement of, and invitation to, this barn party. Juke around your memories of Rex. Evade the day he left you for CSU, the day he left CSU for Lakewood Lumber, for the crunchy blonde bitch he hikes the foothills with and feeds wild berries to. Arrive instead at the root of it all. Arrive at what urged you out of your mother's house, at what drove your ass into that Escort seat, at what laid you down in this truck bed like the dollop of pale, static clay that you are. Arrive at anger.

And stay there. Linger. Inch Odell's left hand to your throat. Listen—

—to Odell's side of the argument, listen to him sweat out a marriage proposal he wouldn't make if not for the news of pregnancy, listen to you crater his proposal, listen to him grow bitter, listen to him lie to his friends about what has made you fat, listen to him hit on Softball Scholarship at the hardware store, twisting pickup lines, tuning them to the offbeat delivery that you once deemed enough reason to advance, that made CUTE and GENUINE gash your brain. Listen to the flopping of skin as Odell fucks Softball Scholarship from behind, listen to him tell her he loves her, listen to her say, I do, listen as their Red Eye lands in San Francisco, or Wilmington, or Seattle, some coastal city promising an opportunity you will never have.

Listen, because this is what you will hear: bile-lathered chunks of granola splashing into toilet water. Your mother screaming as she slaps the shit out of your already blotchy cheeks. The ring-ring-ringing of your last school bell. The glass door of the abortion clinic unlock from the inside. The clunk-clunk of your bicycle's chain as you pedal off, horrified.

Or:

You'll listen as the only cab driver in town demands his fare before you enter the hospital. You'll listen to that thing enter the world. You'll listen to that thing flail in its crib. You'll listen to that thing cry when you tie your server apron straps tight. You'll listen to the lawyer from St. Paul say again that he isn't hungry, and then order his third Tanqueray and tonic. You'll detect the condescending tone in the majority of his words, spliced only by pity. Somehow, that tone will make you consider—actually consider—fucking the fat line cook after your shift. You'll do it. You will. You'll fuck him in the dry storage closet. You'll fuck him hard. You'll get him off within two minutes, you'll go home, you'll go back to work, you'll see just how much he grabs your ass now, how a squeeze has been transformed by sex into, at best, an unintentional graze as he sidesteps for more canola oil. Discarded. Again and again and again.

Listen as you open your server book, to that faint creak, the binding on its last legs. You'll write down an order. You'll close your server book. You'll fulfill said order. You'll open. You'll close. Open. Close. Open. Close.

Listen to that pain. Find its grooves with your fingers and trace it back to tonight, to this very moment.

And feel. Feel Odell pumping faster now—not deeper, faster. Feel the pickup shake. Feel the brisk wind on your raised hands. Feel your anger tendril its way to your shoulder blades. Acknowledge it. But don't shout. Don't whisper. Don't say a word. Suppress it. Suppress it into something you can sidle your nimble hands around. And squeeze. Choke it into urgency.

Grab Odell's thighs and pull him deeper. Increase his pace, too, don't let him resist the strength of your hands. Ignore the synchronicity of his breath and his dick, ignore the two ridges of the pickup bed that are pinching your spine, ignore the, "Odell is fucking some chick over there," from somewhere near the fire, ignore the strain on Odell's face, ignore the new creases that have formed—

—look up at the stars. Turn your eyes into lassos and yank them close. And let go. Let them free. Let him slip out of you. Let him spurt onto your pubic hair. Let him catch his breath enough to muster how great that was. Let him, days from now, when you reject his advance in a janitor's closet, shout, "Slut," from whichever mountain he chooses, whichever ridge can echo a whisper. It will hurt. Somehow, despite what lies you'll tell yourself between now and then—how you stood on that night, how you leapt from the truck bed and walked home in the cold, how you grew, how you evolved—it will. And it should. That pain should make you want to run.

PASS THIS OFF AS LOVE

THAT SUMMER, THEY watered their garden with Super Soakers. Once around 8:00am, and again around 6:45pm, when my parents and I would sit down and search for conversation in our hunks of meat loaf. You've seen it: that grimace on my father's face, that wad of chest hair above the white v-neck he still tugs on each night after work. You've never seen my mother's tools to counter, though: a feigned disinterest scrunching her face, the swirl and sip of cabernet sauvignon, her mind on rough seas but sturdy enough to will the waters still. All the while wondering—perhaps hoping—that my father's scoffs were directed at her, and not the eccentric couple next door.

Looking back, focusing strictly on that summer, strictly on our dinner table, my father could have been scoffing at me. It isn't often that thirteen-year-old boys and their fathers see eye to eye, but especially not when one "ungratefully" ignores the food placed before him and instead gawks out the sliding glass door at what he has convinced himself is greener grass.

My interest wasn't just in how they'd water that garden. It wasn't in how Otto, after strutting across his lawn in his slippers and straw hat, would stand at the northwest corner and calmly pump pressure into the compartments of his Super Soaker before arcing its stream on the zucchini, cilantro and tomatoes. It was how Teegan, at her post in the southeast corner, would look at him. It was how she'd stop shooting, stop pumping, stop whatever she was doing to peek at him through the corn stalk leaves. It was how he'd stare back. It was how, after a moment or two, they would circle one another, maintaining their gaze all the while. Above the rows of carrots, above the broccoli, above all that they'd planted together. It was how Otto wouldn't stop circling. It was how he'd chase her. A man just shy of middle age, playfully chasing. And it was how it wasn't a chase at all, how, instead of running, Teegan would drop the Super Soaker, wrap her bronzed arms around him and then, letting go of the embrace, point to her lips, demanding the last bit of their routine: a kiss. It was love.

Twenty years later, I can interpret Otto and Teegan in this way. I can say now that what I saw was love. That it was genuine. At thirteen, though, I don't know if I really understood what I was watching. A TV show. An odd soap opera. Some play on what I believed to be reality. That said, I still like to think that part of me knew. That my emotional IQ was high and made me wise beyond my years.

"They're the creepiest fucking people I've ever seen," I remember Darren, from across the street, saying. You haven't met him but, that summer, and for a long time after, up until he left Kenosha to study architecture in Madison, we were close friends. We'd ride our bikes together; we'd aim our pellet guns at raccoons terrorizing the suburb's trashcans; we'd spend hours and hours in the tree house Darren's father built, listening to CDs, dreaming of high school, of adulthood, of anything but being a thirteen year old. I believe the tree house is where Darren made that comment. Yeah, that's right. It was there. I remember at that moment having an elevated view of Otto and Teegan in their driveway, setting up for what would admittedly be the most bizarre yard sale I've ever attended—a dozen different sets of Russian dolls, sandals Otto claimed to be woven by Kalahari Bushmen, a US Navy diver's mask, and plenty of other items they had to have known wouldn't sell in a neighborhood as conservative as ours.

When Darren made that comment, though, I didn't know what to say. I didn't know who the creepiest fucking people I'd ever seen were, but I knew it wasn't them. I remember staring at him, silently debating whether I should confess my fascination.

"I saw them naked in January," Darren said. When I turned to him, he shrugged the shoulders he'd soon grow into. No big deal, his shoulders failed to actually say.

"Naked?"

Darren nodded. A certain degree of distress narrowed Darren's eyes then; that look when something you've spent days burying jukes its way back into your brain. "They were out in their yard. Nothing but boots on."

Without my prodding, Darren went on to say that their bodies were streaked in red, something he at first thought was blood but, after a few moments, understood to be lipstick. Smeared across Teegan's face and thighs; thick lines of it on Otto's torso, in the shape of an N, from rib to nipple, nipple to opposite rib, and back up.

In living next door to them for two years, I'd seen nothing like it. But I didn't find myself alarmed by this information. It was gas thrown on my fascination's fire.

"What were they doing?" I asked, picturing a scene not unlike the garden, just without clothes, both playful and primal.

"They just stood there," Darren said. "For five minutes, they just looked at the sky. And then they held hands."

The last time I saw my parents hold hands was years later, when I graduated from high school. You've seen proof of that moment, that framed photo in my mother's den, on the wall, of Darren and I in cap and gown, his narrow eyes and crooked smile aimed directly at the lens, mine angled elsewhere in both pride and confusion at something I hadn't seen for some time, taking place just feet away, on the edge of a handicapped parking space. My mother and father must've been feeling something similar—pride, in me, in themselves, wrecked only by the confusion of how to express that physically, involuntary flutters stabilized by the touch of a partner they know deeply and not at all.

It didn't last long. Twenty seconds or so, a window inched open just far enough for me, and them, to escape. To forget those dinners, the weekends of neglect, of him twirling his welder's mask in the shed, of her phoning her friends in the kitchen and jotting down what they'd list as tent-poles in their lives—where the kids are now, where the next vacation would be, where one could find the best loaf of sourdough. Always, "Where". A profound word for a woman who gave herself no place to go but work, the post office, and the grocery store. Her there, jotting ideas, jotting the lives of others, their evolutions. Poison to her husband.

"Come on, Harold, it'd just be a weekend thing," I can remember my mother saying on multiple occasions, at breakfast, at dinner, before my father passed out in his recliner and snored into the night. It was the only way she thought she could wear my dad down, by promising a trip to be short

"Hell, honey, you know they crank prices up on the weekends," my father would say, followed closely by, "you know I have a lot of projects stacking up anyway," in a tone that suggested my mother had been silly for asking, that she should've known better.

"I know," my mother would say, those rough seas calmed in this instance through repetition: "I know."

Twenty seconds. Twenty seconds and, poof, gone. Like magic. Like a comet overhead, in motion for ages but fleeting to the curious eye straining in the night to see what decades later they won't remember was there at all. That was my parents' love, and the uncoupling of their hands were the last seconds of its pitiful existence.

I went out that night, got drunk at a bonfire, and came home to find them sleeping for the first time in separate rooms. Months later, legs dangling over the wooden frame of my dorm room bunk, I got a call from my mother that, in summary, confirmed that it was over, that my home would become his house and that, at forty-three, she was going to be redecorating her childhood bedroom.

But you know that. And you know how upset I was. What you don't know, what I've only realized in the weeks since Jesse, is that I was wrong in thinking that it was me, their only child, that kept them under the same roof, and able to squeak by as civil. No, what did, what kept them talking, was shared envy—that place where his anger and her sadness could mingle.

Dinner table memories of such:

My father passes along that a coworker made a hefty down payment on a new car:

Mother: "How the hell can they afford that?"

Father: "I guess that's what happens when you stroke boss man's you-know-what."

Or: months before graduation, after Darren announces that his aunt will be paying his tuition, no matter where he goes:

Mother: "That must be nice, you know, not having to worry about all that nonsense—bills, and life, and whatnot."

Darren: "I'm beyond grateful."

Father: "I wish my payscale operated on gratitude."

One or two lines each. That's all, and that's all it would take for one of them to crack a smile, to grab the other's figurative hand and squeeze through that same window of escape. I saw it. I heard it. But it didn't make me sick then like it does now, looking back. I should've said something, done something, complained or set them straight. I should've had the spine to tell them that, together, they weren't good people. Separate, maybe. But not together. Yet I didn't. Not when they coyly ripped on Darren. And certainly not that summer, the night before Otto and Teegan left for a weekend away.

From my bedroom, I'd watched them load their Isuzu in the rain. As far as I could tell—my window being shut after a cold front spun by, my angle too severe, the sky too dark to spot defined facial expressions—no words were said between them. On Otto and Teegan went, from Point A to Point B with luggage, like ants in a colony of two: lift, carry, close door, lift, carry, close door. It wasn't until my parents reached the staircase that I heard any words at all.

Father: "That really chaps my ass, Karen."

Mother: "Which part?"

Father: "That those two dipsticks over there can afford to take off whenever they damn well please. Thunder Bay this time, Otto told me at the mailbox. How? Tell me how, when all summer, all goddamn summer, all they do is fuck around in their yard, shooting their water guns."

Mother: "I know, Harold. I see it too."

Father: "And it doesn't piss you off?"

Mother: "It breaks my heart."

After she said that, the door to their bedroom shut—softly, in sadness, not slammed in anger. I like to think that I spent the better part of that night imagining the dialogue that would continue behind that closed door, but I don't think I did. I doubt I thought about them at all, other than wondering why they couldn't be more like Otto and Teegan. As free-spirited, as quirky, as loving.

###

It was around 7:00am on a Sunday, and I don't know why I was awake. But I was. And there he was: Otto, passed out on my parents' back deck, shorts around his calves, drool pooling on the wood beneath his cheek. An empty fifth of Popov was near his shoulder, its cap somewhere on the dew-soaked lawn.

Most kids, I assume, would've left it at that—hurried upstairs and either woken up their parents or said nothing at all about the incident until years later, over a cup of coffee, or a glass of wine, let the moment breathe, let it transform into a joke, a punchline: "Pants down, dick in his hands, honest to God."

But I didn't look at Otto, even in that moment as something to run from. Nor was I like my parents, who if it had been them that had woken to Otto on their deck, would've snickered over their oatmeal and waited for Otto to rise and look at them in shame. No, as I've made clear to you, I'd come to admire Otto, albeit from a distance. As I've said, he was playful. But he also was careful. He possessed the ability to love things, an attribute I envy still, if only because I fear that neither you or I possess it. What laid before me, I knew then, was the product of something in his life that went awry. Otto needed help. Otto needed to be woken.

And so, as quietly as I could, I, still in my pajamas, opened the sliding glass door and walked out onto the deck. Moisture met my toes; boards creaked beneath my weight; the sour smell of Otto clung to the breeze. Once close enough, I squatted down and poked Otto's bare shoulders. Once, twice, three times. Not a peep from him. Not even a snore.

"Hey," I said. I poked him again. "Hey. Otto. Wake up."

When Otto finally did wake, he had no idea where he was. Didn't know whose deck he'd slept on. Didn't know whose lawn had yet to be cut, whose hands had painted my father's shed midnight blue. He didn't know why his shorts were down. Then he looked at the Popov bottle. He stared at it some more, sat up, ran his fingers through his matted black hair, and redirected his gaze to his own home. The only trees in their yard having just been planted that spring, there was nothing there to fracture the sun, enabling Otto and Teegan's dull green siding in something of a morning glow. At that moment, I remember thinking it looked like a home stumbled upon by weary children trapped in a fable. Without turning his cheek, he called me by name.

"How long have you been standing there?" he asked. His voice was deep, and hoarse, something stuck in his throat, something large. Embarrassment. Still seated, he calmly slid his shorts up over his groin.

"Not long," I eventually said.

"Good." He cracked his neck. "Your parents see me out here?"

"No."

He nodded and then tried to stand, making it only to a crouch before easing himself back to the porch, still drunk. Dizzy. Dehydrated. "Think I can get some water?"

I hurried across the deck, through the door I'd left open, and to the kitchen. I grabbed a glass from the cupboard, filled it, then returned to Otto just as quickly as I'd left him.

"Thanks."

I felt like an idiot standing there, watching him guzzle that water. As if I were witnessing something I shouldn't, a play for which I shouldn't have tickets, an intruder on my own deck. So I turned around, intending to go back inside, to the living room at least, if not to my room, letting Otto leave when he saw fit.

"No," Otto said. "Stay. Sit down."

So I did. I walked closer and, like him, sat on the edge of the deck, my heels on the lawn. We stayed like that for a minute or so, my attention only on him, his on a pair of crows circling his garden. He squinted and, contrary to all I'd seen of him before—the sandals and straw hat, the yard sale circus, the garden games—it made me see him as some character in one of the westerns my father would watch on holidays. The strong cheekbones. The angled nose, the wiry beard. That wounded gaze into what bystanders would interpret as nothing.

"Stupid birds," I said, feeling it to be an appropriate thing to say, an easy way to interrupt the hum of silence.

Otto shook his head. He sipped the water. "They're not stupid," he said. "They're just doing what they do." He ran his fingers through his hair again. "What's stupid is that fucking garden."

I was, of course, surprised to hear this. After a moment, I said, "I like it."

"You want it then, kid?"

"Huh?"

Otto sipped the water. Once, twice. "I'm going to tell you something that nobody else will." He watched the crows. "See, everybody has something to say about love. That's because the experience of love is specific to the individual. Do you know what I mean?"

I doubt I did, but I nodded.

"What people don't tell you—what people say they don't want to talk about—is change." He set the glass down so he could speak with his hands. "Change scares the shit out of everyone, enough for us to declare that we want nothing to do with it. 'I'm happy,' we say. 'I wouldn't want it any other way.'" He dropped his hands. Shrugged his shoulders. The tone of his voice heightened. "But we're lying, kid. We all are. You want to know why?" He waited for a response I didn't know how to give. "Because we change each and every day. We buy a khaki jacket to wear instead of the old denim one in the closet. We go from mop-top to buzz-cut. We shave our faces, and legs, and armpits. We put in premium instead of unleaded." He must've seen then how lost I was. "Let's try this: what kind of soda do you drink? What's your absolute favorite?"

"Orange Crush," I said.

"Okay, so let's say you go to dinner every day. Every single day, you're presented with the choice of Orange Crush, Root Beer and Coca Cola. You think you'd choose Orange Crush every time?"

"For a while."

"But you'd choose something else eventually?"

"Yeah."

"Why's that?"

"I'd get sick of Orange Crush."

"Exactly. There'd be no more excitement with Orange Crush, right? We humans have this innate ability to detect the stagnancy within ourselves, a lack of exploration. We think we're so fucking in tune with it, but we're not. We check the levels day after day after day but we don't know anything about what those levels are saying. Then, without even realizing it, poof, by the time we've actually detected anything, our environment has changed us in such drastic ways that the worry from that detection can only be quieted by drastic action."

If I could go back, if I could, at age thirty-three, sit down once more with Otto and have this exact conversation, I think I'd actually have something to say, something meaningful to add. I'd talk about you. I'd talk about how your ribs continue to swallow your stomach. I'd talk about Jesse. I'd talk about us. We could talk for hours about change. As it was, feeling my young mind to be too inept to contribute, I again opted for silence. I just remember staring at him, wondering if we'd ever be that close again.

"I used to wear a suit every day," Otto said, filling the silence. If he was still drunk, I couldn't hear it in his voice, in his cadence. "I'd wake up, take my favorite coffee mug out of the cupboard and set it on my beautiful granite countertop, put on a pot of French roast, shave my cheeks clean, shower, tie my tie in silence… I used to live in Milwaukee. Had an enormous office overlooking Cathedral Square. Drove this flawless Jaguar for years. Clean, I'm talking clean, kid. Spotless automobile. Used to have friends, too, friends that actually talked about life, about reality, not about what song they've been singing to their lettuce patch."

"What happened?"

"Soda," Otto said. He looked at his house again, at the bay window's blinds being shut. "Soda happened."

I watched Otto track a flock of geese over the treetops, the crows over his garden long gone.

"Ever been in love, kid?" Despite the "kid", he asked this not in a patronizing way, but in a way that somehow transcended our age difference. Like I wasn't too young to have those feelings. Like I wasn't young at all.

I thought I had, and told him so. Explained to him in detail how Bree Higgins walked, how, despite the lisp, her voice made me think of songbirds. I told him how infatuated I'd been with her since 5th grade. And he listened to all of it. He smiled as if what was coming out of my mouth was mending whatever had gone wrong, whatever had driven him to sleep on my parents' deck. He was lost in my words.

"Have you kissed Bree?"

"I can't even say my name in front of her." I couldn't. Funny now, frustrating then.

"It's better that way," Otto mumbled, as if his heart were torn with what his brain had told his tongue to shape.

"I don't know. Just be careful. Sometimes, the closer you get, the more out of love you tend to fall."

Otto handed me his empty glass of water and stood. He stretched like a cat waking from a sun-drenched nap. He thanked me again for the water, and then he was gone, walking across our lawn and into his. Not once did he look at the garden. Nor would he be standing out there that night, or the next morning, Super Soaker in hand, nozzle aimed at the cilantro. The last I'd heard of, or spoken about, Otto was the last time I spoke with Darren, two Christmases ago, over the phone.

We talked about work first. Then his children. Then you. Then his wife. Then college. Then high school. Everything in reverse.

"You remember Otto?" he asked.

"I do," I said. I told Darren that I hadn't thought about him in years, but that wasn't true. Truth is, I still think of Darren and I examining the criss-cross of rubber the Isuzu left on our street that afternoon of mine and Otto's first, and last, conversation.

"I've been thinking about him a lot lately," Darren said. He paused. "Crazy fucker, right?"

"Yeah," I said. "Me too. Crazy."

When I stop to consider love, that's what I return to: two warped examples of relationships I witnessed as an adolescent. I return to slow implosions. Painful, yes, throbbing, yes, but the victims are still functional, for years able to experience brief moments of pleasure, that pain finally vacuumed out by the finality of distance. That's what I return to: to the wounds of others that I've allowed to shape me.

It's only when I go deeper that the murk begins to clear. Because, maybe for the first time in my life, I see myself for what I really am, and have been since seeing my parents hold hands that last time: immovable. Fortified. Unfair. You've tried, for years now, to shove, to scale the walls. I know you have. And I've resisted, but politely enough, and with just enough reason, for you to at first retreat and then return with your invented glimpses of hope: to that vision you still have of me sitting on the front porch of our imaginary suburban home, our sons or daughters lining the top step, sunlight waning while older children pedal by, all voices brimming with joy; Tto the dream vacation you spoke of no more than two weeks ago; to Bruges, pitching me yet again with, "quaint," and, "cozy," and, "romantic"; to when we are old and frail, and it takes both of us to drag a skimpy Christmas tree from the car roof to the living room, but we do it, and it looks like hell, but a necessary hell, our grandchildren there the morning after, still in their pajamas and sliding gifts to one another, indifferent to the eyesore they sit beneath, the bend of its branches, the needles that have fallen and turned.

I know why you believe that man to be me, Chelsea. It's because of where and what we've explored these last seven years. It's because of where we have failed to go. Where I have failed to go. This apartment has become our home, but only because, outside of work, we do not leave. Our friends are gone and we do not visit. We have flown together only once, and that was to be beside your father as he took his last breaths. We don't have enough space to plant a garden. There is no ring on your finger. There is no child in your womb.

This is a scenario that drives a determined woman like you. A canvas with only one corner colored breeds hope: for improvement, for change. And, in grasping for that hope, in grasping for me, you have only changed yourself.

Your hair is short now and, in the past six months, you've dyed it on three separate occasions—blonde, blue, and violet. Each time, you have framed your face with your hands and asked whether or not I like it, to which I have responded: "Yes. I do." In truth, all it has done is make me want it long again, and black, and down, like it was when Grady introduced us.

You wear perfume now. Two different scents, actually, that you alternate depending on what mood you think I'm in.

You're at the tanning bed as I write this.

On the calendar, it says that you have an appointment with a nutritionist next Friday. You wrote it in all caps. You even drew a smiley face next to it.

You want me to notice these changes, to see them as new. You want me to be enticed. Attracted enough to act. You want your changes to change me. But you want me to do so without thought. You want the effect without me knowing the cause. But I have thought, and I have followed, and I have wrestled, and I have dug, more so lately than I ever have.

###

I knew I hadn't looked at you in months. Really looked at you—at your eyes, at your breasts, your legs, nothing. I'd see in your face that you were starting to believe that you were the ghost I was making you out to be. Not seen. Not heard. I caught you looking at yourself in the mirror one night, too, pinching your inner thighs, pulling on your cheeks to deflate the bags beneath your eyes. It made me feel guilt. And pity.

And that's why I came to your office for lunch that day. That's why I carried a bouquet of daisies for thirteen blocks. Because I wanted to do what all other boyfriends do when they realize the love has gone stale and the motivation to find another has run out: lie. But I spent hours convincing myself to believe the lie—the apology, the promises to do more, to get us out of the apartment and into a house, to do whatever it would take to make us happy again. Seeing you like I had, taking the time out of my day to do something I hadn't done in so long, it actually had me thinking it was possible. I could fix us.

So I walked in. I walked past the restrooms, past the drinking fountains, and to the glass doors. The front desk looked empty, unattended. So I opened the doors and veered right, down the hallway that leads to your office. The soft, "Hello," is what stopped me. I turned. Up from behind the desk came Jesse. I said, "Hello" back. She smiled. I smiled. She asked who I was. I told her.

"Oh!" Jesse said. "She's going to love those."

"Think so?"

"Of course she will."

I asked if you were in your office.

She said you were. Then, before I took my second step, she asked, "Can I smell them first?"

To which I said, "Sure," and tilted the bouquet her way.

That's what you saw. That's all you saw. And that's all you wanted to see.

You grabbed your coat. You glared at her on our way out. You tossed your purse against the booth. You barely touched your food. And when you eventually asked, "Do you think she's pretty?" I was anything but surprised. I said nothing. I shook my head. I sternly told you to drop it. And you did.

And that's how we carried on. For three weeks we did, just as we had. Work, home, bed, work, home, bed, work home, bed. One hundred words exchanged, at best, each one generic, each one a fraction of a charade that long ago had lost its meaning. But then, that night—

She was sobbing, Chelsea.

Naked, and confused, and wiping her eyes on our quilt. She sobbed when I took the duct tape off of her mouth and cut the rope off of her wrists and ankles. She sobbed the whole way home, too, no matter how much I apologized, no matter how many times I said, "You won't lose your job over this. You won't. I promise." The sobs stopped only when the interior light kicked on, when she grazed her thumbs over the ropeburns.

And what did you say when I got back? Do you remember? I stormed in to find you in your sweats and over the bathroom sink, brushing your teeth as if nothing had happened, as if it were any other night. You spat into the sink and said to the mirror:

"I'm just trying to give you what you want."

I should've left then, right then, or, if not then, sometime in the night—just waited for you to fall asleep, then tiptoed to the closet, thrown on another layer, and taken off. But you didn't fall asleep that night, did you? What about the night after? I could tell. I said nothing, but I could tell. I still can. A month later, it all continues to eat at you. Your posture says so. Your eyes say so.

And I've had enough.

I've waited far too long, but I must leave you now, Chelsea. I must go far, far away, and I ask only that you leave me be. If you come after me, or try to contact me, I will turn you in. I'll repeat that so that it's as clear as it can be: I will report you to the police if you come after me, if or if you try to contact me.

It's important that you know, though, that I did love you at one time. Very much. But that love vanished as each of our conditions evolved. You see those now, don't you? You have to see it, that what we have is conditional. Your conditions aren't being met. Neither are mine. You buck against that fact and replace it with the notion that you'd do anything for me. But you won't. The lengths you're willing to go aren't for me. They're not. They're for you. They're all for hope. And you pass that off as love.

DEAR HOLLY, BE RIGHT

HOLLY'S FATHER REFUSED to look at her. He glared at the sidewalk instead, at the sky, at pairs of strangers sliding out of minivans and sprinting to the airport's entrance.

"You're hers if you get on that plane," he said. For weeks he'd been saying this. His skin had become sallow. The day before, Holly found clumps of his fine black hair stuck to shower walls.

"I know," Holly said. They'd first had this conversation on the day he decided to show her the postcard, and the week after, while he watched her purchase the plane ticket. It had hurt Holly then. And it hurt her now, being spoken to as some sort of possession making the wrong choice.

"Money's going to be tight."

"I know."

"But you're not going to call me."

"I know."

"Because you're not mine anymore."

"I know."

"If you do find her," Holly's father said, then reached into the bed of his blue Ford pickup, pulling a grey duffel bag from beneath a tarp he'd hooked taut, "I want you to tell her how much of a whore she is. I want you to tell her what I've become, what she's turned me into." He handed the bag over to Holly. It was light, a few pounds at most in the middle, weightless ends curved in the shape of a banana. "I didn't treat that woman right. I didn't at all. But what she did was unforgivable." He cleared his throat. "Can you do that for me?"

"Sure, Dad," Holly said. Lip service.

"And I want you to give her what's inside of that bag."

Holly pictured some sharp object in the bag, a butcher's knife, a piece of glass, something symbolic of how her father now felt, had been feeling. She then pictured herself going through security, being tackled, being detained, imprisoned, stuck in Arizona for the rest of her life, sent back to Wickenburg, sent back to him, to moments just like this. After carefully setting the duffel bag on the sidewalk, Holly leaned down to unzip the main pocket.

"There's a porcelain plate, two pairs of earrings and a picture frame. All of it's wrapped in layers of tissue paper." He waited for Holly to discover this for herself, then: "The things of hers I couldn't toss."

When Holly looked up at her father, when she saw just how hard he was biting his lip, she understood that the anger was only a mask, could only be a mask, and that he was horrible at wearing it. Seventeen years of discontent were torqued between every wrinkle that had formed on his face by age forty-one. And, what had evolved beneath those wrinkles, somewhere deep, Holly knew, was envy. Not just of Holly's mother, for the life she left him for, but of Holly herself. His daughter was leaving. No longer would she have to live in that peanut shell of a home, that love-cursed rambler from which, until now, there seemed no escape. No longer would she have to take long, aimless walks just to feel sane. No longer would she too have to deal with his pain— Hungry Man Thanksgivings on TV trays, weekends spent beer-buzzed, a lawn mown irregularly, when either Holly or her father couldn't hold out for the other any longer and caved. It was his now, all his, only his.

Holly hugged him then, tight. Tighter yet, her tanned face against the Winsol-scented chest of his khaki jacket. If this were it, if this were really it, if he were really disowning her, Holly would miss him. Not his pain; him. His uneven sideburns, the sharp angle of his nose. She'd miss the smell of Simple Green on his hands.

"Dad?"

"Yeah?"

"Am I doing the right thing?"

"You don't get to ask me that anymore."

###

November 14, 2012

Dear Holly,

The last time I saw you, you were just learning to walk. You won't remember this but I used to hold your left hand while you tried to take your steps. Your father held your right and together we'd all inch across the living room. I've been thinking about that a lot lately. Some days I can still feel those little fingers of yours in mine and I can't help but yield to the wave of regret that comes after. And I guess the only thing that I really need to say is that I'm sorry. It's the only thing to say. I'm sorry, Holly. I'm sorry that I left you, that I left when I did. I should've waited until you were older. I should've tried harder. I should've had the courage to come back. I'm sorry.

I'd love to meet the grown you so I can hear about all the steps

you've taken between then and now. If you at all feel the same

way, you're more than welcome in Seattle.

Love,
Kaori

Orange cabs, yellow cabs, white cabs, cabs parking, squealing to the airport's curb, parking, squealing away, in and out like blackhawks evacuating soldiers from a battlefield. One of the orange cabs slammed to a halt in front of Holly. The passenger window was already down, a black man with a thin silver moustache in the driver's seat. "Where you need to be, sweetheart?" he asked with an East African accent.

Holly, after setting the duffel bag and her backpack on the back seat, pulled from her jacket pocket the slip of paper she'd written the address on. "The Freeman Building," she said, afraid she was somehow saying it wrong and, in case she was, providing further clarification, "it's on Cherry Street."

"I'll get you there," the driver said. He tilted the meter toward him, started it, then took off, smiling at Holly's insecurity. "You just relax. Enjoy the ride."

Holly looked at the car's clock. 4:16pm. The Freeman Building's leasing office closed at 5:00pm. She'd digitally signed her lease, and had digitally paid her security deposit. She would've paid her first month of rent that way, too, if she'd had the money then. But, she hadn't, and so she still had to hand her rent check over in order to get the keys to her apartment.

They tailgated the cabs in front of them until they were out of the airport's reach and on the highway. The highway took them over streets dotted with lean evergreens and past vehicles sporting bumper stickers that said, I'M KIND OF A BIG DEAL IN SEATTLE, or showed the cityscape in the shape of an umbrella.

"Does it really rain that much here?" Holly asked. The sky was dark, nearly dusk dark. Somewhere behind all of the slate grey clouds the sun was setting. But it wasn't raining, as she'd been led to believe it did in Seattle, every day. Her father had pointed that out at every opportunity, going so far as to say, "Seattle is the suicide capital of the U.S., you know." Which, following some Google research, she found was untrue. That title belonged to Las Vegas, followed by Colorado Springs and Tucson.

The driver chuckled. "It is January so yes, it will rain more. It's light rain, though, hardly any heavy rain."

"That's the only kind of rain where I'm from."

"From where I am, too." The driver looked in the rearview mirror and smiled. His teeth were the color of sand.

Though she figured he'd welcome the discussion, Holly opted not to bring up Wickenburg. She would not speak of it with pride—the newish library, the dude ranches, the mine. She would not lie and tell him he should visit someday, a mere saloon door to Phoenix. Yet, other than the three times she'd read over her mother's postcard, her hometown had been all she could think about on the flight. Her father. Graduation day. Sneaking onto golf courses at night with Sam, her lover at sixteen, and slitting garden hoses with box cutters.

The driver wiggled into a minor traffic jam on the interstate. Elevated as they were, Holly could see what she knew from online maps to be Puget Sound. Fog over the sea hindered her view of what lay on the other side, what exactly the ferry boats were sneaking toward, looking so small, like toys in a bathtub.

Holly looked at the car's clock. 4:31pm. She wanted to speak up, to let the driver know that there was no other option, that she had to be there by 5:00pm. But she hesitated, not knowing if that was impolite, being so demanding, so uncompromising when clearly there were factors at play out of the driver's control. At least we're still moving, Holly thought.

"So what brings you here, sweetheart?" the driver asked.

There it was. She'd been anticipating that question, dreading it, unable to settle on a surefire response. Three truths had brought her here, to Seattle, to this cab, to this traffic jam. Three truths she knew would inevitably lead to more questions from the driver, but also from anyone with whom she chose to disclose them.

TRUTH #1:
I came here to find my mother.

OUTCOMES (Q & A):
What's she like?
I don't know. She left before my 2nd birthday.

What does she do here?
She could be doing anything.

Where does she live?
My father Sharpied the address on the postcard.

TRUTH #2:
I came here to escape my father.

OUTCOMES (Q & A):
Escape?
He's all I've ever known.

Did he hurt you?
Yes, but not in the ways you're wondering.

What does he do?
Washes windows. Pouts. Repeat.

TRUTH #3:
I came here to find myself.

OUTCOMES (Q & A):
You don't know yourself?
Not at all.

What do you do?
Dream.

About what?
Not feeling alone.

"I need to do something new with my life," Holly eventually said. Something encompassing the three but with enough wiggle room to sidestep specifics in the questions that would ensue. Specifics like those, Holly thought, weren't

for strangers; they were for the Sams of the world; they were
for mothers.

"You seem young for a middle life crisis, sweetheart,"
the driver said. The traffic jam eased into motion within
seconds, a white-gloved police officer waving vehicles
around a rolled silver Impala. "How old are you?"

"Nineteen."

"No, no, no, too young. Much too young." They were
back up to seventy-plus miles per hour now, passing vans
struggling to shift from second to third, approaching
overpasses on the outskirts of downtown. Skyscrapers came
into view, and stadiums, and buses. "Nineteen is not for
worries like that. Nineteen is for having fun, for dancing, for
singing, for making money and kissing boys." He took the
next exit, which looped west, toward Puget Sound. "You
know what I mean, sweetheart?"

Holly didn't. She'd never understood why people
discuss youth as if it were something to be tossed around
lightly, as if choices at ten, or twelve, or nineteen do not
have consequences. Choices of impact, Holly believed, could
be made at any age. A life of meaning didn't have to start
after a childhood of jackassery. Holly hated the wide margin
of error given to children and teens and young adults. She
saw it as farcical, even, the way young people were on one

hand encouraged to live it up and make mistakes, and, on the other hand, expected to be better than anyone that had existed before them—farcical, and sad, the set up for failure. There remained a part of Holly, however, that worried the true fuel of this discontent was jealousy—that her margin of error had been far narrower, that her depressed father had hardly encouraged her to do anything, especially to make mistakes.

Holly didn't see the point in arguing with the driver, though. Relax, the driver had even said himself. And she wanted to try. Point A to Point B, she thought. "I understand," she said, then let silence sprawl its tense wings from window to window.

The next five minutes went on with the cab climbing and descending sloped streets while Holly, cheek pressed to the window, attempted to take in street names. Yesler and Spruce, Boren, Fir, and Alder. She gawked at monuments, at the skyscrapers, considering the care that had to have been taken in constructing such things. She pictured wrecking balls and cranes and high school graduates tiptoeing high beams, shaping the skeletons of these buildings with hammers and torches.

Then there were the faces. Attractive faces on bicycles, beaten faces dragging worn soles, wide eyes, narrow eyes, angled eyes. Black, white, tan, phantom-like, translucent. Faces beneath turbans, beneath bandanas and poet caps, above scarves and neckties and herringbone coats, homeless faces resting on cardboard stories. Diversity lived here, Holly had told herself while still in Wickenburg, and now saw with her own eyes. Mobility lived here. Resurgence was possible here.

They eventually double-parked on a west-facing down slope. Ahead, through a narrow break in the fog, Holly spotted mountains her aisle seat had prevented her from seeing on her descent. Not the rounded mounds of soft rock and clay she and Sam had hiked over in Arizona, but mountains. Upwards of 5,000 feet. Real mountains, travel guide mountains, snowcaps. She pictured her apartment high enough to breathe them in as she woke.

"Which one is the Freeman Building?" Holly asked. Each immediate building looked the same to her: short, narrow and bricked either red or yellow.

The driver pointed to the south side of the street, at a yellow building with a short staircase and a glass door. He tilted the meter toward her. "$47.50, sweetheart.

Holly's stomach split, the bottom half sinking, the top half stretching to her throat like wet dough. Idiot, she thought, you fucking hick idiot. Quickly she reached into her backpack and pulled out her wallet. Thirty dollars. A few quarters, some pennies. Her father had given her an extra $15 to check the duffel bag he'd given her, but $15 hadn't covered it and Holly had had to dip into her own cash.

"Sir," Holly said. She cleared her throat. "Sir, I only have thirty dollars."

The driver rubbed his face as if he'd been expecting that response, as if he'd bypassed anger altogether and only disappointment remained, not in her, but in himself, in having laid the groundwork for the acceptance of mistakes. He reached over into the passenger seat and shifted loose papers around, as well as a stack of paperbacks from the library, searching for his credit card reader. No luck. He moved his travel mug out of the cup holder and searched there but, still, nothing. Not in the glove compartment or the center console either. He sighed. "Let's go to the ATM then."

Holly looked at the car's clock again. 4:48pm. If they searched for an ATM, she could miss getting into the Freeman Building entirely. She could be on the street for the night, or at a hotel whose nightly fee would gouge what little money she'd saved. "I don't have any time to go to an ATM," Holly said. "I'm so sorry. I know you don't have any proof, but please believe me when I say I'm good for it. I'll be here for six months—that's how long my lease is. At least six months. I'll be right here, sir, in this building. I'll see you again."

"This is a big city, sweetheart."

"I know, but—but come back tomorrow even and I'll be able to pay you the difference." Now, more than she had in the past five hours, Holly wished she'd begged her father for his truck. Hands and knees begged, I'll-call-her-a-whore-as-many-times-as-you-want-me-to begged.

"Wait," Holly said, brightly. "I have checks, I can pay you with a check—"

"I don't accept checks."

"Do you have a business card then? Here, give me your business card and I'll call you."

"I don't have a business card." The cab driver sighed. "Why didn't you just take the light rail?"

Holly had no clue what the light rail was. She'd never heard of such a thing. Fucking hick. Tears came on, confused tears, panicked tears, soundless tears that, had he not looked in the rearview mirror, the driver never would've noticed.

"Don't cry, sweetheart," he said. "Please, don't cry. You need the money for food, yes? And for a toothbrush and such?"

Holly nodded while wiping her eyes.

"Now you know how much it costs to take a cab. Correct?" He waited for Holly to nod, then said, "Public transit is good here. Best option if you're on a tight budget." And finally, as he cleared the meter, more to himself than to Holly: "Consider your first cab ride in Seattle my gift to you and your new life."

Holly slid her inflated air mattress across the hardwood floor and against the wall, its plastic lining sounding to her like a cat sharpening its claws. There were deep gouges on the hardwood, assumedly from previous tenants dragging recliners and sofas and tables and ottomans, from one corner to another. 265 square feet in all, one bathroom just barely larger than a bookcase, a lone east-facing window in the kitchenette that glimpsed some cluttered apartment across the alley with a vase of wilted roses on the windowsill. Though each eggshell wall was dry to the touch, they, as if the maintenance crew had turned the apartment that morning, smelled of fresh paint.

Holly knew that she shouldn't like the space. She knew that she shouldn't look at it and think to herself that the

$850 check written upon arrival was well spent. It was run-down. There were water spots on the ceiling shaped like dead tree branches. Each light bulb gave off a different tint, dim yellow to near-blinding white and back to yellow. But the place was hers. Hers. Hers!

Much could be done to make 265 square feet unique, she thought. Matching black leather furniture, glass tables, bright red rugs. As she'd been picturing since Sam, her first apartment would be made modern. Clean, straight lines. Sleek. Little, if anything, on the walls—framed aerial photographs of Arizona, successive as if telling a story of her journey, her roots. But that was all. Because this wouldn't be a place to dwell on the past. No they'd think of the future here. This wouldn't be a place to sit for hours on end and binge TV shows, but a place for she and her mother and her friends to breathe, to recuperate after hiking those western mountains, to prepare for a night out in gorgeous dresses, sipping from stemmed wine glasses.

Soon, Holly told herself. Soon enough, that day would come. First, she had to get a job. And on days off from that job, she'd use time and money to find her mother. She'd go beyond the fruitless Google searches, beyond the dollars and moments to be wasted on the most recent edition of the phone book. She didn't know how exactly she'd do it, but she'd find her mother. And everything else would follow.

Soon, she reminded herself. She then eased herself onto the air mattress and reached for her unzipped backpack, from which she pulled a laptop. Once open and running, Holly searched for available networks not requiring a password for access. BROCKER50791 was the only one without a chain icon. Holly clicked on it. Access granted.

Forget email, forget Facebook; she immediately went to Craigslist. seattle/tacoma > jobs > food/bev/hosp. Dozens of positions listed just that day. FT/PT servers, AM/PM cashiers, dishwashers, bartenders, bakers, bussers, baristas, barbacks, Beecher's Cheese cutters, so many words starting with a B, so many damn words in front of her, opportunities for her to smile at. She couldn't help but smile. She couldn't stop smiling. She'd spent five days in Wickenburg perfecting her résumé, drawing as much attention as possible to her three summers as "Busser/Server" at Harvey's BBQ, to that one full year as "Front Desk Clerk" at the Scorpion Tail Inn. Snagging a 'getting-by' position, Holly felt, was going to be easier than she'd initially thought. She had references, good references. For God's sake, she had Harvey Preen III himself to attest for her punctuality, her willingness to learn, her communication skills. He'd said it himself the day she told him she needed to work full-time, year round, that she was taking the job at Scorpion Tail: "We're going to miss you, Holly."

In the same clothes she'd worn the day before—denim jacket and tight black jeans—Holly walked across Cherry St. toward her apartment building, clutching one paper bag filled with items she'd been too busy to buy before nearby stores closed: a throw pillow, a blanket, toothbrush, toothpaste, deodorant, shampoo, toilet paper, a shower curtain, a day-old (and half-off) baguette she planned to gnaw on throughout the day. In her other hand was the folded cash she'd just withdrawn from the 7/11's ATM; she'd taken out $40 that she planned to stick in an envelope marked DRIVER—THANK YOU, along with fifteen dollars she'd already had. She didn't know if, or when, she'd see him again. But if she did, it was important to her to be ready. It was important to her to properly say thank you. She stuffed the cash into her pants pocket as she continued walking.

Last night, Holly had slept for maybe two hours. Tossed and turned, either too cold, too excited, or too foreign to the noises blanketing her in the night. Sirens, car alarms, an offbeat drip/drizzle sonata in her tub, drunken shouting down on the street. From the apartment above her, no later than 6:00am: the pitter-patter of a small dog's paws, the vibration of a treadmill at walking speed. None of it had angered Holly. Not even as she stared down a distorted version of herself in her building's glass door. Her hair was greasy and matted. Her clothes were wrinkled, skin and lips dry but not yet cracking. She scratched plaque from her front teeth and wiped it on her jeans, then unlocked the door with her key, anxious to be free of the filth she'd allowed to form.

Holly saw that Michelle's office door was open. Some bass-heavy techno track from her computer's speakers overpowered the ringing of her work phone. The few times she'd spoken to Michelle on that phone had led Holly to believe that Michelle was pushing forty. Her voice was deep, calm, soothing, a slight rasp at the end of each word that Holly felt hinted at jazz clubs, at Boulevardiers, and escapades. Which is why it had surprised Holly the day before to see that Michelle was nowhere near forty, but closer to twenty-five. She had long legs and kiwi green eyes, short black hair and the cutest freckles strung across her cheeks like bistro lights. Michelle was Sam; Sam, with more lines on her face, and slightly darker lips. Sam, with smaller ears but just as much soul. Michelle was beautiful. Holly had never felt right walking away from beautiful.

Michelle sat behind her chaotic desk, finding elbow room somewhere between staplers and sticky notes, her head propped by a flat palm. The phone kept ringing. One ring, two rings, three. Michelle seemed to reach for the phone, though the movement turned out to be a mere stretching of a kinked wrist. It took her a moment to spot Holly and, when she did, it took one more moment for her to a) turn her music down and b) remember exactly whom Holly was.

"There's my newbie," Michelle said. "How was your first night?"

Holly clung to 'my newbie', imagined it as a cartoonish bubble growing out of Michelle's mouth, 'my' italicized. "Good," Holly said. Somehow, despite the reality of how it had been, Holly, in Michelle's presence, was convinced that this was the truth. "It was good."

"Sit, sit," Michelle said, waving Holly to one of two chairs in front of the desk. She had on black and white striped mittens, fingers buttoned back to the knuckles. Bad circulation. Whisper: Baby, I'm cold. "Finding everything okay? Having any trouble with the buses?"

"No trouble at all," Holly said. Which wasn't true. She hadn't taken a bus, hadn't spotted a stop that didn't house hard women with jagged teeth, or men scratching at their forearms and obliques, at scabs on their shins. Truth was, other than field trips, Holly had never stepped foot on a bus. Carpools. Bicycles. Walks. Her father would pick her up after work. He'd mumble about his day, chug what remained of the Sprite he'd been nursing, pull into the nearest gas station for a new case.

"I'm glad," Michelle said. "If you get a chance, you should head up to Ballard."

Ballard sounded familiar, as if it was a word Holly should've taken note of weeks ago, when researching Seattle, reading up on the neighborhoods of Queen Anne, and Wallingford, and Fremont, picturing her mother as either a businesswoman in a pantsuit living blocks from the Space Needle, or a woman in homemade overalls, sharing a commune in the treetops. Maybe her cab driver had mentioned Ballard. Her face apparently gave away her mind's pursuit.

"It's my favorite neighborhood," Michelle said. "Quaint, lots of cute little shops. There's this one coffee place, Penelope's. My friends are crazy about it."

"Are you crazy about it?"

The rasp carried over to her high-pitched laugh; a chickadee with a cigarette. "I mean, I like it. Yeah, I like it. Well, it's okay. I tend to spend more time at bars than I do at coffee shops." She gave Holly a look that said she knew saying such a thing was mischievous and it made Holly wonder if Michelle spoke to the rest of the tenants in the same way—even the elderly men and women Holly had seen stepping into the elevator on her floor—or if she was slick enough to adjust for all, for each age bracket. "There's one I go to often called The Viking's Head that I think would fit your vibe." Michelle wrote the name on a sticky note and handed it to Holly.

Which confused Holly. Michelle had seen Holly's driver's license. She'd made copies. Nineteen years of age was on file, somewhere, everywhere. Still, Holly thought, she was to burn no bridges, especially that extending to the striking woman across the desk she felt guilty both staring at and looking away from.

"I'll have to check it out," Holly said. "Thank you."

"You're very welcome. Seriously, if you need anything—a recommendation, directions, whatever—you know where to find me. I've gotten to know this city pretty well."

At this moment, Holly considered asking Michelle if she'd ever encountered a woman named Kaori Porter, or if there was anyone on her extensive contact list that had, someone to guide Holly toward one of the things for which she'd come to Seattle. But there'd be questions. Deep questions, and the deep would turn dim, and then dark, darker than Holly was willing to go with Michelle here and now. Broken, dislocated, irreparable: the last things she wanted this woman to think of her.

"Where are you from?" Holly eventually asked. She guessed California, then Florida, places Holly thought responsible for producing beauty.

"Indiana," Michelle said, and scrunched her face as if the word alone made her nauseous. "Don't even ask." She waited for Holly to finish laughing, then: "Lived with my brother for a while in the U District, at least until I could get on my feet. Do you have family here?"

Holly thought of her mother, of the postcard, of the family portrait she'd watched her father smash when she was five. How even then, with her baby daughter in her arms, her mother had looked unsure of herself, a crooked smile, that scar above her right eyebrow sloppily covered by makeup. She wanted to tell Michelle her mother's name. She wanted to tell Michelle stories she'd never been told, about her mother's Japanese heritage, about her mother's family, that they were pure, divine. But Michelle's phone rang once more, this time seemingly twice as loud as before.

"I'm sorry," Michelle said. "I should probably take this though."

"It's no problem," Holly said, and stood. "We'll talk soon." And they would. Holly would make sure they would.

###

A day later, the first response came. Fractured gray light bled through the kitchenette window. Holly sat cross-legged on her air mattress, holding her Pop-tart to the side, careful not to get crumbs on her keyboard.

Dear Holly,

Thank you for your interest in the position of Barista. Unfortunately, we have decided to move forward with the application process without you. We do, however, encourage you to apply to more positions through our esteemed company as they become available. Best of luck in your job search.

Another, near dark:

Dear Holly,

The next morning, two more responses came that said the same exact thing: "Unfortunately, we have decided to move forward with the application process without you."

Rattled wasn't the right word to describe how Holly felt. Neither was confused, or furious, or defeated. Glum, maybe, melancholic. Deflated, like a tire, like a balloon mistied and released into a clear sky but now tumbling back to earth. She'd been rejected before, but not like this, not this way, through emails sent by strangers, complete strangers who'd glanced for eight seconds at titles and bullet points and dragged her documents to a digital folder labeled NO.

How much easier it was, Holly thought, to be denied by those close to you. How much easier it was to have her father, a man who had watched both her strengths and flaws evolve, condemn her decision to fly to Seattle. How much simpler it had been for Sam to take Holly's fingers out of her and walk off of the sixth green—a par-three—into town, to Evan, who she'd days later hold hands with down the hallway, eyes on her knees, her gorgeous fucking knees.

Pathetic. That was the word. Pathetic, to the point of lying on her back all afternoon, in her underwear, on her air mattress, still the only piece of furniture in her studio. To the point of taking half an hour to listen to the tenant above take a shower, all the while watching the water stains on her ceiling grow toward one another, three branches with intentions of convergence. Pathetic to the point that, instead of searching for and applying to more jobs, all she could bring herself to view online was her bank account. $417.78. Groceries, the public transit card she'd loaded in order to avoid carrying so much coin.

She wanted to scroll through her contact list and call Sam and confess to her how pathetic she was for still thinking of her three years later, for still wanting her. She'd define the word for her, she'd explain its origins, she'd use it in five sentences for her if it provoked Sam to say some version of, "I'm sorry," in that timid voice, the S and long O shoving themselves through that twig-wide gap between her front teeth, "For leading you on, for making you chase."

And she wanted to call her father. With limited minutes, of course, he'd agreed to keep her flip phone on his plan. "For two months," he told her. "Two months is all I'll give you. After that, you're on your own."

But she thought maybe a call now would be worth it. It wouldn't matter which words he chose to use—"You are pathetic", "Fuck you"—or if he was drunk, or which tone the words rolled along. She wanted to hear his voice. She wanted to know if he was ready to tell her the truth about her mother. Not just, "She's a whore," or, "She didn't like us," or, "She's a whore that didn't like us," none of the vague, overused excuses, no more dodging, no more hiding, no more suppression.

"Did she really fuck other men?" Holly would ask him. "Did you beat her? Is that how she got that scar? Is that what drove her to Seattle? And why Seattle? Why didn't you say a goddamn word about Seattle? Why, Dad? And why would you cross out the address? I know why. You don't want me to find her because you know she'll tell me that you beat her into fucking other men. Isn't that right?" She pictured herself gasping for air, saying in under a minute what she hadn't ever been able to say to his face. "Or was she like me? Huh, Dad? Did she like women? Was she guilted into dating you, into marrying you, into making me? Huh, you persistent fuck? Huh? What makes a woman a whore?" He wouldn't say a word. She wouldn't let him. Because she'd have an epiphany, right there, phone pressed to her cheek. "You're pathetic. And you've made me pathetic.

Click.

She'd hang up. She'd feel euphoric, but filthy, as if she were atop an oceanfront dune, wind whipping sand into her hair and pores. She'd clean herself, and what then? Back to the air mattress? Back to sending out her résumé? Within an hour, within a day, within a week, all signs back to pathetic?

Best to conserve the minutes for phone interviews, Holly thought.

She rolled off of the air mattress and stood, conscious of but ignorant to the popping her stiff joints made. She hurried to the duffel bag she'd placed against the opposite wall, picked it up and walked into the bathroom. She sat on the toilet and unzipped the duffel. Bundled in one bulky, wretchedly-taped package were her mother's items. Holly tore into the tissue paper, hearing the pearl earrings roll across the surface of the plate. She'd never seen these things, hadn't known her father had hung onto something of her mother's. Where had he kept them? Under his bed? In his toolbox? Somewhere in his packrat closet?

Earrings in hand, where he'd hidden them no longer mattered; they were beautiful, even in the dim yellow light of her apartment. Two pair, one small, one much larger, gaudier, but both studs and with gold stems. Holly set the earrings gently on the kitchen counter and lifted out of the duffel her mother's porcelain plate.

Rectangular and with a white base, the plate's design was of a giant oak with a rope swing dangling beneath its thickest branch, a child swinging parallel to the ground. Intricate, Holly thought. Beautiful. Her mother was beautiful. Her mother was a beautiful creature, some beautiful creature her ugly father damaged. At first, she could barely stand to look at the framed photo beneath it all, the earrings and plate. It was a school picture of Holly, age eight, and so much of her was her father: those big hick ears, a miniature but angled hick nose, a thin hick mouth. Of her mother, she'd been given light tan skin, dark hair and eyes. And it still wasn't enough. Those missing teeth should've been her mother's. That faintest of scrapes on her chin from when she fell off of her bicycle should've been her mother's. If her mother had been there, she never would've worn that ugly Yosemite Sam sweater. She never would've sat before that photographer with frizzy hair. She never would've ended up here, in Seattle, not in this way, on a toilet seat and pathetic.

###

CL>seattle>for sale/wanted>jewelry
PEARL EARRINGS—GOOD QUALITY

Can sell them to you individually ($75 for the small, $100 for the larger), or as a set ($150). I'm no jewelry expert but, as you can see in the pictures, both sets of earrings are in good condition. If you'd like to see more pictures, just ask. If you're interested in buying, please respond. I'll be in touch shortly after that. Thanks, and have a great day!

-Holly

Immediately after opening the Freeman Building door, Holly heard a man yelling. Muffled but still vicious; a rabid dog with the cage door locked. She found herself gravitating toward the yelling, leaning an ear closer and closer to Michelle's office. At first, Holly thought that Michelle was gone for the day, sick or otherwise, her substitute taking himself too seriously over a conference call, or unable to control his emotions with a repeatedly destructive tenant. But then, briefly, there was her voice.

"Get your fucking hands off me, you fuck!"

Holly opened the door. Over Michelle's desk stood a thin white man with baggy gray chinos and a short, wide mohawk. He was young, younger than Michelle and, upon noticing Holly in the doorway, he took his hands from Michelle's wrists. He turned to Holly. His eyes were denim blue, and bloodshot. Michelle rolled her chair along the wood floor, away from him.

"Hey Holly," Michelle said, damp eyes communicating something of gratitude for the interruption. "Did maintenance look at those water stains yet?" She cleared her throat. "Did they?"

Holly had mentioned the stains to Michelle but hadn't formally submitted a maintenance request. This was an act. "Yeah," Holly said, walking closer to the desk, "yeah, they took a look at them." The man smelled of gasoline as he walked past her. There were dark stains on his light green jacket, flecks of white paint on the sleeves. He slammed the door behind him and only then did Holly ask Michelle: "Are you okay?"

"Oh, that?" Michelle said. Her eyes fluttered about— ceiling, desk, floor, wrist. She forced a smile. "That was nothing."

"Are you sure?" She considered saying something else, something more. That wasn't nothing. Considered pressing for information, for the identity of the man, for the basis of he and Michelle's relationship. Deterring him from violence,

Holly felt, should result in such information. She deserved that. At least that. She wondered if he was an ex-lover, a former tenant, a former employee, even a friend who frequented Penelope's, someone Michelle had unintentionally crossed. Because Michelle would cross no one willingly. She couldn't. Look at her. Vulnerable looked even better on her than confident.

"What can I do for you, Holly?"

Something in the way Michelle asked that question signaled to Holly that playtime was over. She'd been looking at her black and white mittens. She'd said it slowly, and with gravel in her voice. As brief as it'd been, no longer would they sit in this office, or anywhere else, and flirt. It would be too embarrassing for Michelle. Holly had thrust herself into something she never should've seen, something Michelle probably never wanted her to see. And neither could go back.

"I was wondering if you had any postcards laying around." Which was true. If she couldn't call her father, she'd mail him, at the very least let him know where she can be reached.

"I think so," Michelle said. She walked to a trio of filing cabinets against the back wall and opened a drawer.

Everything about her body language said she no longer cared. "Choose which one you'd like."

Holly walked over, looked in the drawer, chose the most generic one she could, with the Space Needle Warhol-ed on the front. She nodded her gratitude at Michelle and walked toward the door.

"Here," Michelle said, "You'll need a stamp." She ripped one from the book on her desk and handed it to Holly. The Liberty Bell, cracked.

"Thanks," Holly said.

"Look, Holly—"

"It's fine," Holly interrupted. "Just let me know if you need anything, okay." She knew Michelle wouldn't, that she'd swallow whatever it was, even teeth and blood, before further exposing her problems to this just-met transplant. Yet, Holly felt it needed to be said, and was pleased to have Michelle meet her words with a smile, fake as it was.

###

Dear Holly,

I'm interested in both pairs of earrings. I'd really like to get a look at them before I commit to $150 though. That's nothing against you. Just want to make sure they're right for daughter. I look forward to hearing from you.

Sincerely,
Zayra

Dear Holly,

*Thank you for your interest in the position of Barback.
Unfortunately, we have decided to move forward with the
application process without you.*

Dear Holly,

*Thank you for your interest in the position of
Administrative Assistant. Unfortunately, we have decided
to move forward with the application process without you.*

Dear Holly,

*Thank you for your interest in the position of Courtesy
Clerk. Unfortunately, we have decided to move forward with
the application process without you.*

Dear Zayra,

*It was so nice to meet you and your daughter today! She's
such a cutie and I'm so glad she liked the earrings. That's
all I wanted to say, really. Please do let me know if you need
any help at the art gallery. Would be more than happy to
offer my services. Take care!*

Sincerely,
Holly

Dear Holly,

Thank you for your interest in the position of Customer Service Representative. Unfortunately, we have decided to move forward with the application process without you.

Dear Holly,

Thank you for your interest in the position of Cleaning Assistant. Unfortunately, we have decided to move forward with the application process without you.

Dear Holly,

Thank you for your interest in the position of Sales Rep. Unfortunately, we have decided to move forward with the application process without you.

Dear Dad,

Hope all is well. Thought you might like to have my address on hand. So, there it is. Things are going great here. Meeting a lot of nice people, enjoying the scenery. Call me if you'd like.

Love,
Holly

Dear Holly,

It was so nice to meet you too! Isn't she precious!? Me and Vern can't get enough of her. As for the gallery… We aren't currently seeking help but that doesn't mean we can't work anything out in the future. Maybe in 2-3 months? That'd probably be the earliest. I'll talk to Vern about it sometime soon and get back to you. Sound good? Forgot to say this earlier: Welcome to Seattle!

Sincerely,
Zayra

CL>seattle>for sale/wanted>household items
FLAWLESS DESIGNER PLATE FOR SALE

One of a kind Japanese plate that has never been used. Has been passed down through my family for generations. $475 OBO. Needs to go soon. If you'd like to see more pictures, just ask.

-Holly

###

From her window seat on the 40 bus, Holly watched the sunlight burn through yet another grey morning. It seemed to turn Lake Union back to blue, what leaves remained on damp trees to green. Cyclists came out of hiding, weaving through traffic fast enough that their silver breaths trailed instead of led. The bus approached a stop in the Fremont neighborhood. Several on the bus stood, neck strained, eyes down at their phones, headphones on. They danced around one another in a somewhat orderly fashion toward the exits, which, considering how no one had said a word, Holly found remarkable. As they filed off, aboard came several more, occupied, eyes down, mouth shut. Replaced, not entirely unlike Michelle had been.

Giovanni Brenko, late thirties and with slicked brown hair, had been in Michelle's office chair for the past eight days. He smelled of chicken nuggets and Old Spice and had a thick nose and the wide-set eyes of a mustang, near oblivious of what stood before him unless he turned his head. He answered the phone on the first ring. He listened to The Carpenters, seemingly on repeat. He'd treated Holly as if she were twelve.

"Portland," Giovanni had said, and slowly, speaking of his roots. "It's a city in Oregon. Oregon isn't too far from here. It's a state along the Pacific Coast."

Empty-handed Holly stood in the leasing office, nodding, knowing within seconds of meeting him that there was nothing she could do to change the narrative: he'd always think she was this dumb.

"Is there anything else I can help you with?"

"Yeah." Holly paused then, maneuvering a way to ask what was on her mind without offending Giovanni. "Has Michelle been relocated to another property or—?"

"Well," Giovanni said, crossing his arms, "I'm not at liberty to discuss that." He leaned back in Michelle's chair. "And do you think you should be worrying about where she's gone?"

Holly shrugged. Bit the inside of her cheek to keep from thinking of how much she hated being spoken to like this. "I mean, she's a human, so yeah, I think it's okay to worry."

Holly had multiple times pictured that man strangling Michelle with a piece of rope in a dimly lit park, leaving her for a different man to find and defile. She pictured that man beating Michelle's temples with a book as thick as his thigh, then slamming it on her kidneys as she fell to the ground. Holly had even splurged days earlier and purchased a copy of the Seattle Times, relieved to not find a Michelle of any kind in the obituaries.

"Well," Giovanni said, visibly frustrated. "I assure you that Michelle is safe and healthy."

"Northwest Market Street," the bus's automated voice announced.

Holly tugged the cord above her. A ding sounded through the bus, registering her request. When the bus came to a complete stop, Holly, eyes open, ears uncovered, backpack tight on her shoulders, exited, then walked two and a half blocks west, where, there, on the north side of the street, stood Penelope's.

On one wall of the coffee shop hung a painting of an elephant with disproportionate tusks. On the opposite wall was a mural of some prairie, a blurred cheetah hunting a gazelle, a lion lying nearby, colorful birds overhead, some others perched on the lone tree in the center. Against each wall sat leaning customers, whispering customers, old customers, young customers. The aroma was aggressive, as if Holly had just jammed a slit coffee bean up each nostril.

A barista with the complexion of blond wood wiped the counter as she spoke to Holly: "You're gonna be glad you came in today." Her forearms were muscular, but not too muscular, defined, but not overtly so—strong and attractive as she gripped that cloth.

"Why's that?" Holly was at the counter now.

The barista held a smile that gave away just how happy she was Holly hadn't avoided her trap. "Well, today, and just for today, we're offering a reduced rate on what we call Tiger Fang. Have you ever heard of it?"

Holly hadn't, and said so.

Spot on, in rhythm, the barista said: "It's a dry-processed Ethiopian blend that you'll find has both citrus and floral accents. You'll also find hints of jasmine and cocoa, pineapple and rhubarb." The barista paused, either having forgotten what came next in her pitch, or trying to let her awkward yet confident silence do the rest of the selling. She eventually caved. "It's to die for," she said.

"It's really that good?"

"Babe, it's the best. Would you like to try a sample?"

Holly nodded, watched the barista release some Tiger Fang into a fluoride cup and bring it over. Babe. She'd never been called that, by anyone. Holly took a sip when the barista returned. She'd liked coffee since she was thirteen or fourteen, but had never loved it. Enough to not settle for instant coffee, but not enough to frequent coffee shops. And so she immediately questioned herself, her tastes, and her status when she thought the Tiger Fang was good, not great. She could taste a hint of citrus fruit—something acidic, at least—though she wouldn't classify it as pineapple. Otherwise, it tasted like coffee. Like really, really strong coffee. She took another sip.

"It's like sex, right?" the barista said. Whatever she did with her eyebrows—a raising of them, a lowering, what was it that she did?—hinted at Holly that she'd been having plenty of it.

Holly smiled. "I'll take a small cup."

"That's my girl," the barista said. She turned around, grabbed a clean eight-ounce coffee mug. "That'll be four dollars, babe."

Four dollars? Four dollars!?

The barista's smile, as well as her general air of friendliness, disappeared once the sale had been verbally made. Despite her internal objection, Holly handed over her four dollars and, Tiger Fang in hand, Holly walked to the middle of the coffee shop and sat at a table for two facing NW Market St. Four dollars. Four fucking dollars. Holly unzipped her backpack and pulled out her laptop. While the machine warmed, she watched squinting flannels walk past the front door, and peacoats, V-necks and beards and stocking caps. Some even wore sunglasses, their eyes anything but accustomed to the winter sunlight. After she connected her laptop to Penelope's WiFi, Holly logged in to her email account.

Dear Holly,

I am very much hoping your plate is still for sale. Even now, when I'm supposed to be working, I can't help but look at it

*and be transported back to my childhood. Such a gorgeous
thing it is. I will say upfront that $470 does seem a little
high for me. That doesn't mean that it doesn't have value,
just that the highest I think I'd be able to go would be $425
or so. Would that work for you? Please do let me know.
Talk to you soon.*

Sincerely,
Donald Koh

Holly opened another tab and logged in to see her bank account. $471.46. She had two weeks before the month turned. The absolute lowest she could take and be able to pay for another month of rent was $379. Take the $425, Holly thought. You'll be able to cover the electric that way, too. You can do that. You can go two weeks without spending a dime. There are some crackers left. And a can of tuna. A few bites for each meal. You've got this.

Holly returned to Donald's email and hovered over the "Reply" button for a few seconds before clicking. She wondered if she could hold out any longer, if she'd be making a mistake by setting up a meet-and-greet. She wondered if somewhere out there her mother was scouring Craigslist for something totally unrelated to the plate, but somehow, somehow she soon would stumble upon the ad, see the picture, see it signed "Holly" and lose her breath, catch that lost breath, reply. Meet. Hug and cry, cry and hug, help Holly pay rent, help Holly find a job, offer Holly a place of comfort, solace, do her part in ending this struggle. But it was wrong. Holly knew it was wrong, to expect a miracle. Wrong to think that her mother would somehow find her, wrong to doubt, even for a second, that the only move she could make was to buy time.

> *Dear Donald,*
>
> *Thanks for the reply! I'm so glad you're interested in the plate and that it allows good memories to be re-lived. I really would like to get $400 out of it but*

Just then Holly was distracted by a pregnant woman with wet hair being pushed past the Penelope's entrance by a skinny man in a hooded sweatshirt. He was yelling at her as he did so. She was in tears. The whispers within the coffee shop ceased altogether, all eyes on the entrance, all asses in seats. Holly thought of Michelle. Holly thought of her mother, pictured a young, drunk version of her father angry about what would later be thought nothing, but shoving— just shoving, shoving-shoving-shoving Holly's mother across the sidewalk, into a building, into traffic. And then something in Holly's gut turned, churned, boiled, roiled, did something with just enough force, just enough power to stand her up and walk her past all of Penelope's seated onlookers, cup of Tiger Fang in hand.

"You can't take that cup outside," the barista said.

But Holly opened the door with her free hand. Out she walked, to the skinny man, who was now waiting to cross the street. She tapped him on the shoulder and, before he could turn entirely around, Holly flung her Tiger Fang all over the left side of his face. Steam rose from his cheeks. He howled, some hybrid of coyote and man, a howl that intensified as he pressed his fingers to the blotches. Holly hoped that it wouldn't end, that his burnt face would blister, that it would be gawked at by passersby, that his stubble would smell like coffee for days.

And then, her eyes still on the man, Holly was shoved to the side. Again. And again, until balance was lost.

"What the fuck, bitch?" the pregnant woman yelled at her. Her breath smelled like gin and Juicy Fruit gum. Tears would not stop falling from her eyelashes. She repeated it as she shoved, both her hands and her words gaining power: "What the fuck, bitch?"—shove—"What the fuck, bitch?"— shove. The only thing that deterred her from her pursuit of Holly was the groaning, coffee-covered man who had curled himself on the sidewalk, to whom she waddled to and said, "Baby, are you okay? Baby?"

Holly watched as the pregnant woman helped lift the skinny white man to his feet. They walked east on Market St. together, toward nothing but the same. He would beat her for this. In his eyes, it would be her fault. And maybe it was, Holly thought. Maybe she was in the wrong, staying with him, encouraging a lost cause to be a better man, birthing his child, something that would link them together for the rest of their existence.

Holly went back inside Penelope's, back to whispers. She returned the empty cup to the barista, then packed her things, exited, and stomped west on Market St, until she could go no further. Up 34th Ave. she went, north as the sky closed back into layer upon layer of gray, up steep inclines with no purpose other than to walk, just walk, until her lungs hurt, until her thighs burnt, past an arts and crafts store, past burgers and fries, past fish baskets and king salmon stew, past other things she could not afford to try, past rundown video stores and seasonal ice cream parlors. She walked until she heard starving seagulls begging for bread in Sunset Hill Park.

Elevated hundreds of feet, Holly looked down on Puget Sound. It was calm. There was a marina crowded with sailboats. Cars and vans and trucks inched toward what appeared to be a beach further north. The smell of saltwater was on the air. Fifteen feet from her was a bench positioned to take full advantage of the view. Holly walked to it. She allowed a smiling family of four to pass on foot before sitting down. And there she'd sit, for hours, waiting for the gray to dissipate, all to see those westward peaks on the other side, doing what she could to slow her breathing, to shove what had transpired out to sea.

###

The tears came moments after Donald Koh left her apartment, and they weren't alone. Screams came, incoherent screams, violent screams into her air mattress, into the throw pillow she'd bought weeks ago. $300. That's all Donald—wiry, preppy, kind-eyed Donald—had offered after twice insisting it was a plate of Korean origin, not Japanese, after running his fingers along the dings on the backside of the plate, dings Holly had never noticed but could not dispute. $300 because he could hear the tears forming first in her throat. $300 because he saw her as a charity case, yet another thing she could not dispute, a girl unable to attain what she wanted on her own, a girl not to hug but to give money to. Because his $300 would fix it all; it's all he could comprehend as possible. She cried and screamed for that, for being pathetic, for the knots of shame in her stomach. She cried and screamed for the mother she desired but did not know, in intervals, in short bursts, cheeks slipping on the plastic covering of her air mattress.

Half an hour later, Holly was on her side, silent, listening to the elevator in the hallway go up and down. Neighboring doors opened and closed, footsteps back and forth, voices coming and going. She was convinced that she was the only person in Seattle with no place she had to be. Work. A friend's house. A lover's bed. Her family home. Nothing, nowhere. Yet that was not the catalyst for the second wave of tears. What choked Holly was the reality that she would soon be homeless. Adding Donald's money to her savings, and even depositing the cash she'd withdrawn for the cab driver, still meant that she'd be short on rent. There would surely be a warning before eviction. But a hole was being dug, one from which Holly knew the climb would grow steeper and steeper and steeper. She pictured herself hitchhiking back to Arizona, thumb plugged into the sky, but who would stop? And what would they demand? And what could she trade for those miles but her body—this fucking air mattress? Could she trade her body now, on the street? For $50? For $100? How far could that get her? The only choice she felt like making in this moment, the only thing that made sense, was to cry. And to scream.

For five minutes more, she let it out, more than the first wave, higher, deeper, body coiling like a snake around warmth, gnawing at her pillow, until an incisor punctured the air mattress's casing. Air wheezed out of the hole as she wiggled. Then she cried harder, she screamed louder, and louder, and louder, stopping only when there was one loud knock at her door.

Holly sat up. More air hissed out of the air mattress. She wiped her eyes. And she waited. And she listened. Thirty seconds later, there was another knock, and another, two parts of a rapid series, pop-pop, pop-pop.

"Yeah?" Holly said. Her voice, as congested as it was, cracked.

"My name is Janet LeVitre," came from the other side of the door, high, slightly shrill but muffled. "Are you okay?"

"I'm fine."

"I don't think you are." A moment of silence passed. "My name is Janet LeVitre. I am your neighbor. I live directly above you and I am concerned. I'm not leaving until I see that you're all right." She immediately resumed her knocking, making it abundantly clear that she was not in the business of bluffing. Pop-pop-pop-pop-pop-pop, pop-pop-pop-pop-pop, pop-pop-pop. And on, and on.

When Holly had had enough, she rose and opened the door. And there stood Janet, fortyish and lean, short hair dyed white, large glasses swelling what Holly would notice later were beady eyes. She had braces with alternating green and red bands.

"Thank you," Janet said. She followed Holly into the apartment, conscious not to shut the door behind her, it being her only escape route. Janet took in the studio's emptiness, the bit of gray day allowed in. "Did you just move here?"

Holly plopped onto the air mattress. Air wheezed out. She nodded and sniffled and rubbed her reddening eyes with her fingertips. "From Arizona."

"Very cool," Janet said, "I grew up in Salt Lake City."

Despite wanting someone—anyone—in her life, Holly didn't care. Now, exhausted and embarrassed, was not the time. Here, in this wasteland of a studio, was not the place. She hoped the silence would drive this woman out.

Janet folded her arms and walked around the studio like a mother would, not necessarily judging, but inspecting, poking for fixable blemishes. She looked at the framed photo of young on the floor, in her Yosemite Sam sweatshirt, and smiled. Then at the ceiling, at the water stains. "Holy shit," she said. "If we don't get that fixed, my tub's going to fall next to your bed." She turned to see Holly wipe her eyes. "Look, I don't know what's troubling you, and I don't know if I'd act any different if I were in your shoes, but I want you to know that I'm only here to help. Do you understand?"

"Yes."

"And I can't help if you don't tell me what's wrong. Do you understand that?"

"Yes."

"Can you talk about it?"

"Yes." Holly still couldn't bring herself to look at her for any longer than a glance. In flashes, she watched Janet cross the room, to the air mattress. When she plopped down, a large gust of air burst open the hole Holly had created earlier. The air mattress sank slowly to the floor.

"Ahh," Janet said. "Here I was thinking you couldn't stop farting."

Holly smiled, briefly at first, but soon found herself losing ground. The smile turned into a laugh, the laugh into a giggle, the giggle into tears, the tears into sobs. She was hysterical and she rested her head on Janet's shoulder.

"Oh, honey," Janet said. She wrapped her arm around Holly and pulled her close, the shoulder of her yellow t-shirt dampening gold. An old man carrying a bag of groceries stopped near the doorway and stared at the two of them until Janet waved him off down the hall. "You just talk when you're ready, okay?"

When Holly was ready, she told Janet everything. Sam, her father, her mother, Michelle, employment, Craigslist, Penelope's, everything.

"Giovanni might be able to give you an extension," Janet told Holly.

Holly's words were still punctuated by tears. She'd talked to Giovanni that morning, before Donald Koh stopped by. "He told me it was out of his hands."

"Well, fuck him then," Janet said, shaking her head. "We'll figure it out."

###

"You've reached Steve. Sorry I can't make it to the phone right now but if you leave a message after the beep, I'll get back to you as soon as I can."

Beep.

"Hey Dad," Holly said. She paced Janet's kitchenette in khaki pants and a light blue t-shirt with the tag still on the collar. Dirty baking dishes were piled in the sink. Sepia-toned photos of a small boy in Spider-Man sweatpants hung on the refrigerator door. An old terrier named Roscoe weaved between Holly's steps. "I just wanted to let you know that I'll be starting a new job tomorrow at a shop called Brocker's. It's west of Seattle, on Bainbridge Island." Holly couldn't remember what else she'd been planning to say. In the silence, she leaned down to pet the dog. "Anyway, that's all, really. I hope you're doing okay. Call when you can." She paused then, long enough to feel her stomach turn. "Love you.

After she hung up, Holly walked into the living area. Janet was seated in a rocking chair near the window, needling the first stitches of a pink and blue scarf. "Aren't you glad I made you do that?"

"I guess." Holly was, though. Even if he never called her back, Holly was okay with picturing her father listening to that message, incapable of uncurling a smile.

"Of course you are," Janet said. She set the yarn and needles on the floor, then stood up and slipped on her turquoise windbreaker. "You ready to go?"

"Where?"

"The shop." Janet grabbed a hefty set of keys from the nail they hung on.

"I don't start until tomorrow, do I?"

Janet smiled. Her teeth looked like Christmas. "No, but you need a lay of the land."

###

Aside from the wake of the ferry, Puget Sound was quiet, crisp. The sky was split gray and blue, the sun peeking through in spurts. The ferry continued to pick up speed. The islands—what had appeared from Seattle as gradual mounds of green—grew larger by the second, docked sailboats bobbing in the water, stone houses extending out of those green mounds, their chimneys puffing smoke. Behind it all were the Olympic Mountains, those westward mountains Holly had stared at so often, had longed for. It was calming, she found, the view. Her heartbeat was slower, her face and jaw and neck with as little tension as she could remember them having.

"Sounds like a freak show, right?" Janet said, referring to the shop she owned, a café-slash-trinket-slash-gift-shop-slash-art-gallery. "For the longest time, it moved with me and my ex-husband. St. Louis to Tulsa, Tulsa to Santa

Barbara, Santa Barbara to Portland, blah, blah, blah. All over the place. I sold coffee out of cars, paintings out of vans, anything I had, really."

Holly watched tourists on deck snap pictures of one another. Families with selfie sticks. "Was that your maiden name? Brocker?"

Janet joined Holly in leaning on the railing. "Brock was my son's name." As if she knew Holly would have questions, Janet continued without pause, without so much as a blink: "He turned six before he was run over by a semi-truck. Doctors said it had to have been close to painless, something that large squashing something so small, you know?"

Holly pictured it: a summer day, an elevated street, a stray ball, and Brock, cute and blonde and curious, chasing, just chasing that ball. She could feel him go under the tires.

"I'm so sorry, Janet."

Janet smiled. "I know you are, sweetie." She kept her eyes on the various birds circling the ferry, flying in loose formation as if guiding the boat to shore. "But it wasn't anyone's fault. It really wasn't. Brock was clueless, the driver was busy. Things collide, Holly. Things collide and we feel sorry about it, sometimes for years." Janet faced Holly, dry-eyed, comfortable. "Eventually, we grow tired of feeling sorry. And, when we stop, that's when we truly act, that's when we do great things."

"That's when you named it Brocker's."

"It was L & J's before. The L stood for Leon."

"Your husband?" After Janet nodded, Holly asked: "Where is he now?"

"Don't care," Janet said. "Haven't talked to him for years. Even before Brock was killed, he and I were going to shit. He knew it. I knew it." She kept her eyes on the water. "And I was a wreck, Holly. No, seriously. That's the only word for it. Wreck."

Holly pictured a thinner Janet, a hungrier Janet, a sharper Janet, pointed not just at her elbows and wrists, but at her shoulders and hips. A brunette Janet wrapped in a quilt, looking through bedroom blinds at the sunrise.

"When he said he was going to divorce me—God, it was only months after Brock—when he said that, something came over me. Sadness? No. Frustration? No. Just straight to anger." Janet stared at Holly. "I went after him with a meat tenderizer. We lived in West Seattle at the time and in that house we had this great big living room window. And that's where Leon went after he told me he'd be divorcing me. He just walked away from me and kept his back turned. In the kitchen, we had all of our utensils hanging, and I grabbed the thing closest to me. I squeezed that thing tight, and I went after him. But that's all I remember. To this day, that's it." She then inched her windbreaker sleeves to her forearms. "As I inched out of the blackout, the first thing I remember seeing were the handcuffs. The first thing I heard was the dispatcher's voice over the radio—no clue what she said, something riddled with code. And, the first thing I felt? The first thing I felt, believe it or not, was relief. That I was going somewhere. And that someone was taking me there."

Once the initial shock of Janet's story passed through Holly, empathy triumphed. She placed herself as much as she could into Janet's shoes, into that relationship, into that scene, into that trauma, that hell, finding herself amazed at the outcome, at who the person before her had become. Yet, Holly looped again and again around one question, knowing then, understanding the glaring difference between she and Janet:

"Why didn't you leave Seattle?"

At which Janet smiled, and pointed to Bainbridge Island, then back to Seattle. "Brock still lives here." Silence. The circling gulls. "He loved it, Holly. Absolutely loved it. The water, the mountains, the parks, the shops, you name it." What Janet did next—not so much of a nod, but a tilt of her head—allowed an expression in her eyes that declared what she was about to say was perhaps the most honest thing she ever would. "I still live for him."

As she looked at Janet, there was some unexplainable ping in Holly's gut that she took as a message. This, it said, at least for now, is exactly where you are supposed to be.

Holly touched Janet's arm and, though she questioned she could say it with as much certainty as she'd desire, said, "You're a good mother."

###

One Space Needle keychain, one Pike Place Market keychain, and two posters of Bob Marley, one in concert, one where he's kicking a soccer ball. After she rang the items into the cash register—her fingers had become like a pianist's: active, spidery, never searching for combinations or rhythm, but knowing exactly where she'd left them—Holly placed all items into one bag and handed it to the mother standing on the other side of the counter. She, like her husband and programmer son, who were horsing around near the exit, wore a black Microsoft cap and a white Xbox t-shirt.

What came next, after the transaction and generic "Thank you, have a great day," had, in three weeks, become

Holly's favorite part of the job: the mother would walk to her family, turning around once, and only once, to get another glimpse of Holly. Boldly, she'd then announce in front of all souls in the store that the girl behind the counter was cute, and friendly, and that the son should ask her out. The son's face would turn pink. He'd wipe his sweaty hands on his jeans, and shake his head, the expression on his face one not of rejection, but indecision, and fear, of doing so in public. He'd back his way out of the store, and the mother, the sweet mother would give Holly a look that was both an apology and a promise, that the son would be back. And then, a quick smile and wave from the father, and they'd be gone.

The whole display would make Holly smile. She felt like she was doing everything right—the tasks of her position, the customer service, even her look: the bit of make-up she'd been putting on, the smile, striking enough for both mothers and sons, even if it led to her politely declining. Emerging from the storage room behind the cash register was Greta, carrying a small box of magnets she was to place on the twirling display twenty feet away, near the east wall. Greta was a part-timer who shaved her own head, had piercings from eyebrow to chin, and wore a facial expression that projected only a fifth of the attitude she truly had. Often she refused to wear the uniform, the pink and black argyle polo shirts Janet had chosen because of how hip she (mistakenly) thought they looked. Instead, Greta would show up in long-sleeved t-shirts, sometimes even sweaters, something with enough length to conceal the palm tree tattoos on her wrists—points of embarrassment.

"Saving money to get those fuckers removed," she'd said on Holly's first day.

Greta wasn't someone you tried to steer, uniform code or otherwise, especially if you were Janet. At twenty-six, Greta had been a baker before, she'd been a barista, a cashier, even a custodian. She was a jackknife Janet could place anywhere.

As she set the box on the counter, Greta saw Holly's lingering smile. "Jesus, another one?"

"Another one," Holly said.

"Send him my way next time, would ya? This gal's bed has been far too cold." Greta nudged Holly with her elbow and smiled. She cracked her neck, then looked out past the counter, at the one elderly regular, Mrs. Kroiberg, who was holding a t-shirt to her chest, deciding whether or not the size would fit. "What a slow damn day."

"Slow damn week," Holly said.

"It'll pick up. You just wait—come summer, you'll be wishing for days like this."

Before Holly could respond, jogging across the store was Janet, hand securing the ridiculous baker's cap to her head, flour handprints all over her dark blue shirt. "Girls!" she yelled. "Girls, I'm experimenting!"

"What has gotten into her?" Greta mumbled before Janet reached the counter.

"I need your opinion, girls. I either want to make chocolate chip banana muffins or this Irish coffee recipe I've been meaning to try. I'll make both eventually but what do you want right now?"

Greta: "Chocolate banana."

Holly: "Chocolate banana."

"Chocolate banana it is," Janet said. "We'll make the Irish coffee muffins later," Janet said to Holly, then winked. And, like that, she was off again, jogging through the store.

Greta watched Holly for a moment, noticed a subtle shake of her head. "That wink though?"

"It's nothing," Holly said.

"That shake of your head said it was something," Greta said.

She had to tell her. If she didn't, Janet would. Later today, tomorrow, next week, sometime soon it would surface. "Last night, Janet asked me to move in with her," Holly said. Over tomato basil penne and merlot, she had. She'd said that Seattle was expensive, that she saw Holly as a daughter, that they were basically roommates already and that little would change if they searched for an apartment together, a loft out of Giovanni Brenko's grasp.

"Are you going to?" Holly had expected a cackle rivaling a hyena's, but Greta asked this sincerely.

"I told her I'd think about it."

Greta nodded, then picked up the box of magnets. "I think you should." Before she walked around the counter and to the twirling display, she added, "If you don't, fuck it, I will. How could you not love that woman over there?"

And Greta was right. How could she not? If it weren't for Janet, Holly would be on the street, or back in Arizona. And Janet was still saving her: Janet had for a month of Holly's rent, for all of Holly's new clothes, for all of Holly's public transit fare. Janet took Holly grocery shopping, then made Holly's meals. Bought her shampoo and conditioner, makeup and nail polish. They'd gone to movies, they'd grabbed coffee, they'd seen Alonzo Bodden together at Parlor Live. "At least until you're on your feet," she'd said to Holly, slipping the doorman a $20 bill to bypass their assigned seating for the front row, something she claimed was because she hoped the two of them would be ribbed by Alonzo himself.

Tender. Thoughtful. Generous. Three words Holly knew she'd use to describe Janet if asked, but three words that, though she couldn't fully comprehend why, had begun to instill within Holly a fear she'd never known: that she was being had. That Janet's charity was not a product of altruism, but perhaps a series of selfish acts with one goal: to redistribute the weight of the son she'd buried, to set it upon Holly, her new brace.

Recalling the condition Janet had found her in, Holly began to blame her worry on the speed of it all, on she and Janet's trajectory, on the fact that she herself could not accept without hesitation what she'd desired for so long— something good, something wholesome. This shouldn't be happening to me, Holly had thought, time and time again since meeting Janet. I don't deserve good things.

Holly looked at Janet then, in the café portion of the store. Watched her toss a small ball of dough at Frank, a distant cousin of hers she'd flown in from Lyon after seeing on his Instagram stories just how skilled he was with desserts. She laughed. She returned to mixing something in a large glass bowl. She couldn't stop smiling.

I have to move in with her, Holly thought then. I owe her that much. I have to.

"Excuse me, miss?" It was Mrs. Kroiberg. She was at the counter, looking every bit of seventy-three and wafting a lilac scent as she walked. Once she saw Holly was out of her daze, she held up a gray and orange t-shirt that said, DON'T !^&* WITH SEATTLE. "Do you have any mediums back there?"

"Let me check for you, Mrs. Kroiberg," Holly said, then went into the storage room. There were boxes stacked on the floor—more magnets, more keychains, more Christmas ornaments, puzzles and board games. Above the boxes was a clothes rack whose center was bowing, sweaters and jackets shoved to the sides to compensate. Holly flipped through the t-shirts, checking tags, finding a medium DON'T !^&* WITH SEATTLE. "I found it, Mrs. Kroiberg," Holly announced. But, when she walked through the storage room doorway, it was not Mrs. Kroiberg she saw.

At the counter was an Asian woman wearing gray business slacks and a collared purple top. If it weren't for the few wrinkles around her eyes, Holly would've guessed she was in her early thirties. Her black hair was in a ponytail, an unsure smile pulled across her lips and cheeks. There was a scar above her right eyebrow.

"Hi Holly," Kaori said. Her voice was low and dense but smoother than Holly had imagined. Velvety.

Still in the doorway, Holly felt her stomach rise, then fall, then rise again. Her mouth went dry. She could not blink.

Mrs. Kroiberg, who had yet to move, slowly merged into Holly's line of sight. "Were you able to find a medium, dear?" She held out her hand as if expecting it to be met with the shirt. "Can I see it, at least?"

Greta, understanding that something was off about the situation, put the box of magnets in her hands down and hurried over to the counter. "I can help you, Mrs. Kroiberg." She stared at Holly before and after taking the t-shirt from her hand. "Everything okay?"

Holly blinked. Holly nodded. There were no tears but she wiped her eyes anyway. Her mother smiled at that. "Hi," Holly finally said, stepping toward the counter. She wasn't sure what came next—What are you doing here? How can I help you?

Kaori stepped closer to the counter, spoke lower. "Your father said I could find you here." When she saw how confused the statement made Holly, she pulled one piece of folded paper from the black purse she kept on her shoulder. "He said you've been in the city since January."

Holly nodded, then took the letter from her mother. Her father's tiny, jagged handwriting was all across the page.

"He also said it was his fault you haven't been able to get a hold of me." Kaori cleared her throat. "Of course he didn't feel that an apology was in order but—but that isn't important. What is important is that you have my information." She set a different slip of paper on the counter, one with her address and phone number, then shook her head. "I know you're at work; I don't expect you to drop everything and come with me right now. That'd be incredibly unfair of me. But, I'd love it if we could get together, have dinner, grab tea, catch up. Whatever you'd like."

Holly, still numb, looked from her father's letter to her mother's eyes, from her mother's eyes to the letter. She looked at Greta, at Greta talking to Mrs. Kroiberg, from Mrs. Kroiberg to Pierre and, finally, to Janet, who had taken off her baker's cap, who now stared at Holly in confusion, wondering if it was an unruly customer Holly was dealing with, someone needing to speak with the owner, someone needing to be straightened out by overwhelming kindness.

"Holly?" Kaori waited for Holly's attention, then said: "How does that sound?"

Holly folded the letter. Hand it back to her. She did. Move your feet. Smile. "That sounds good," she said, surprised at how composed her own voice was, how strong, how impenetrable. "I'll call you when my shift is over."

Kaori smiled. She placed the letter back into her purse, slung the purse back over her shoulder and, before walking toward the exit, said: "I look forward to it."

Holly then took her mother's information from the counter and stuffed it into her pants pocket. She took in her surroundings: Greta still chatted with Mrs. Kroiberg; Pierre worked some dough; Janet was on her way over.

She'd ask Holly who that was, what the woman wanted, and Holly would say, "That was my mother," and Janet would nod, and maybe she would wink, and Holly would smile, all afternoon she would smile and, when her shift was over, when another day was done at Brocker's, she'd punch out and, while walking to the ferry with Janet, she'd call her father. She'd call her mother. Then, she'd go home.

ABOUT THE AUTHOR

Garrett Francis is the author of the novel *And in the Dark They Are Born* and the short story collection *Strays Like Us.* He grew up on a small farm in Michigan and earned his B.A. in Creative Writing from Grand Valley State University.

In 2012, Garrett co-founded *Squalorly*, a digital literary journal of the Midwest and served as its nonfiction editor until 2014.

In 2016, founded Orson's Publishing in 2016, a micro press and served as the press's sole editor (and designer, and publicist, among other roles) until its closure in 2020, publishing four book-length works by new and emerging authors.

He also founded *Orson's Review* in 2017, a digital literary journal that served as a companion to its parent press, publishing fiction, creative nonfiction, poetry and photography. He served as the sole editor of *Orson's Review* as well, and is proud to have helped bring the work of over 70 international contributors to life.

Today, Garrett lives in the Pacific Northwest. Short works of his have been published in literary journals like *Midwestern Gothic*, *Barely South Review*, *Whiskeypaper* and *Monkeybicycle*.

###

Visit authorgarrettfrancis.com to learn more about Garrett and his work.

ALSO BY GARRETT FRANCIS

And in the Dark They Are Born

www.ingramcontent.com/pod-product-compliance
Lightning Source LLC
Chambersburg PA
CBHW011032190726
48290CB00011B/2804